Longarm glanced at Hollis. Hollis glanced back, melting snow sliding down the conductor's round spectacles. Longarm drew a breath and strode forward. He took a lantern, tramped to the far side of the room, and headed for the man in the shadows.

Uneasiness plucked at the short hairs along the back of the lawman's neck. Holding the lantern high when he was ten feet from the man in the shadows, Longarm realized why. He'd thought he'd been unable to see the man's head because of the deep shadows on that side of the room. But he'd been wrong . . .

. . . The man's head was not in its rightful place atop his shoulders. Instead, the head was resting in the man's lap, cradled in his large, dirty hands . . .

DON'T MISS THESE
ALL-ACTION WESTERN SERIES
FROM THE BERKLEY PUBLISHING GROUP

THE GUNSMITH by J. R. Roberts
Clint Adams was a legend among lawmen, outlaws, and ladies. They called him . . . the Gunsmith.

LONGARM by Tabor Evans
The popular long-running series about Deputy U.S. Marshal Custis Long—his life, his loves, his fight for justice.

SLOCUM by Jake Logan
Today's longest-running action Western. John Slocum rides a deadly trail of hot blood and cold steel.

BUSHWHACKERS by B. J. Lanagan
An action-packed series by the creators of Longarm! The rousing adventures of the most brutal gang of cutthroats ever assembled—Quantrill's Raiders.

DIAMONDBACK by Guy Brewer
Dex Yancey is Diamondback, a Southern gentleman turned con man when his brother cheats him out of the family fortune. Ladies love him. Gamblers hate him. But nobody pulls one over on Dex . . .

WILDGUN by Jack Hanson
The blazing adventures of mountain man Will Barlow— from the creators of Longarm!

TEXAS TRACKER by Tom Calhoun
J.T. Law: the most relentless—and dangerous—manhunter in all Texas. Where sheriffs and posses fail, he's the best man to bring in the most vicious outlaws—for a price.

→→→ **TABOR EVANS** ←←←

LONGARM

AND THE
HOWLING MANIAC

JOVE BOOKS, NEW YORK

THE BERKLEY PUBLISHING GROUP
Published by the Penguin Group
Penguin Group (USA) Inc.
375 Hudson Street, New York, New York 10014, USA

Penguin Group (Canada), 90 Eglinton Avenue East, Suite 700, Toronto, Ontario M4P 2Y3, Canada
(a division of Pearson Penguin Canada Inc.)
Penguin Books Ltd., 80 Strand, London WC2R 0RL, England
Penguin Group Ireland, 25 St. Stephen's Green, Dublin 2, Ireland (a division of Penguin Books Ltd.)
Penguin Group (Australia), 250 Camberwell Road, Camberwell, Victoria 3124, Australia
(a division of Pearson Australia Group Pty. Ltd.)
Penguin Books India Pvt. Ltd., 11 Community Centre, Panchsheel Park, New Delhi—110 017, India
Penguin Group (NZ), 67 Apollo Drive, Rosedale, North Shore 0632, New Zealand
(a division of Pearson New Zealand Ltd.)
Penguin Books (South Africa) (Pty.) Ltd., 24 Sturdee Avenue, Rosebank, Johannesburg 2196,
South Africa

Penguin Books Ltd., Registered Offices: 80 Strand, London WC2R 0RL, England

This is a work of fiction. Names, characters, places, and incidents either are the product of the author's imagination or are used fictitiously, and any resemblance to actual persons, living or dead, business establishments, events, or locales is entirely coincidental.

LONGARM AND THE HOWLING MANIAC

A Jove Book / published by arrangement with the author

PRINTING HISTORY
Jove edition / April 2010

Copyright © 2010 by Penguin Group (USA) Inc.
Cover illustration by Miro Sinovcic.

All rights reserved.
No part of this book may be reproduced, scanned, or distributed in any printed or electronic form without permission. Please do not participate in or encourage piracy of copyrighted materials in violation of the author's rights. Purchase only authorized editions.
For information, address: The Berkley Publishing Group,
a division of Penguin Group (USA) Inc.,
375 Hudson Street, New York, New York 10014.

ISBN: 978-0-515-14781-0

JOVE®
Jove Books are published by The Berkley Publishing Group,
a division of Penguin Group (USA) Inc.,
375 Hudson Street, New York, New York 10014.
JOVE® is a registered trademark of Penguin Group (USA) Inc.
The "J" design is a trademark of Penguin Group (USA) Inc.

PRINTED IN THE UNITED STATES OF AMERICA

10 9 8 7 6 5 4 3 2 1

If you purchased this book without a cover, you should be aware that this book is stolen property. It was reported as "unsold and destroyed" to the publisher, and neither the author nor the publisher has received any payment for this "stripped book."

Chapter 1

"Where the hell's Longarm? I'm a-gonna fee-lay the hog-wallopin' son of a bitch!"

Deputy United States Marshal Custis Long, known far and wide to friend and foe as Longarm, lifted his tongue from the cherry-red left nipple of the lovely youngest daughter of the banker of Amarillo and said, "Damn, if that don't sound like Thunder Brodie, I'm a monkey's uncle and your hand ain't wrapped around my pecker, Miss Nancy."

The sweet but not so innocent Miss Nancy Plaza unwrapped her fist from Longarm's ironhard shaft and widened her cornflower blue eyes in shock and alarm. "Oh, for goodness sakes! Who is that scoundrel, Marshal Long?"

The thundering baritone made the lamp chimneys tinkle as the man shouted through the floor from the main saloon hall below the lawman's rented room in the Palo Duro Inn, "I know you're up there, Longarm. A little bird told me!" Thick, rumbling laughter—the guffaws of a man who'd consumed at least one bottle of low-grade hooch. "Get down here and face me like a man, you law-bringin' son of a bitch!"

Longarm studied the deep valley between Miss Nancy's plump, pale, bell-shaped breasts and nodded slowly. "Yep. That's who it sounds like, all right. Thunder Brodie."

He ran a thoughtful hand down the girl's right thigh spread winglike out over the edge of the bed, making way for Longarm's hips. "Or the ghost of Thunder Brodie, I should say. I thought for certain I'd shot and killed the son of a bitch last week—the third of the four ring-tailed polecats that robbed your daddy's bank, Miss Nancy."

Longarm nibbled his longhorn mustache and shook his head again, thoroughly befuddled by his own, uncustomary negligence.

"Longarm!" the booming voice bellowed once more. It sounded as though Brodie or whoever Longarm's caller was had crossed the now-silent saloon to shout up the Palo Duro Inn's broad, carpeted stairs. "You hear me, Longarm? I done come to get my reckonin'! You killed my pards, and you damn near killed me! Now I'm gonna kill you sure and true, and I'm gonna feed your carcass to Mrs. Willoughboy's hogs! Anyone tries to stop me, they'll get the same!"

"Yep," Longarm said with a sigh, running his hand from the banker's comely daughter's porcelain-smooth thigh to give her dimpled chin a little affectionate nudge. "It sure is Thunder Brodie. I'll be damned. Thought I left him dead in that deep box canyon on Black Mesa. Bobcat supper, don't ya know? Hard to believe the crazy bastard would follow me back here to Amarillo, the scene of the man's many sundry and nefarious crimes. But that's Thunder Brodie, all right. Crazy and unpredictable."

He chuckled as he ran his gaze down the girl's soft, supple body, all but revealed by the blue silk dress Longarm had managed to unlace, unbutton, pull down, and push up, discovering after twenty minutes of strategic maneuvering that she'd come visiting his room under cover of darkness, using the hotel's back door and stairs, wearing not a single stitch of underwear.

"Oh, Custis!" the girl said, framing his face with her hands and staring up at him in horror. "He sounds just *awful*! What're you going to *do*?"

"Longarm!" thundered Brodie's voice from the first floor, causing the lamps and windows to shake once more. "I'm gonna give you just ten seconds! And then I'm a-comin' badge huntin'!"

Longarm leaned down to kiss the girl's pale, pink-tipped right breast, which glistened in the room's umber lamplight with saliva that the lawman had worked around it with his tongue. He'd fancied such a frolic with the tawny-haired daughter of George Plaza since he'd dined at the banker's brash digs two nights ago, in celebration of the lawman's securing the fifty thousand dollars in cold, hard cash that the Brodie Bunch had unceremoniously lifted from the vault of Plaza's bank at high noon about three and a half weeks ago, leaving two clerks as dead as wizened panhandle fence posts.

The girl had nudged Longarm's boot under the dining table that celebratory night and then caressed his thigh until she'd all but slipped a hand inside the fly of his tight, tweed trousers, getting her point across until he

nearly came in his pants. Miss Nancy Plaza might have
looked as though she spent all her time behind the baby
grand piano in her parents' stately music room, dressed
in white lace, dancing shoes, and hair ribbons. But she'd
mostly definitely learned from somewhere how to stoke
a man's broiler, and it was clear as the apple cobbler and
whipped buttery cream on Longarm's dessert plate that
the fair-haired child had wanted to fuck.

Now Longarm bent down and pressed his lips to
the seventeen-year-old's warm inner thigh, causing her to
shudder and sigh. Then, with a reluctant groan, he dropped
his stockinged feet over the edge of the bed to the floor
and cursed under his breath at Thunder Brodie's poor
timing.

"Miss Nancy." He sighed, heaving himself to his feet
and tucking his still-jutting hard-on back through the
open fly of his balbriggans, which, working himself up
slowly by chewing on the girl's nicely shapes breasts and
nuzzling her cinnamon-furred snatch, he hadn't quite
gotten around to shedding just yet. "I reckon I'm gonna
go ahead and finish the assignment my boss, Chief Marshal Billy Vail, sent me all the way down to Texas for in
the first place and which I came dangerously close to
leaving open, with a wild, kill-crazy bank robber scot-
free!"

"You better call for some help, Marshal Long!" the
girl urged, pushing up on her elbows but leaving her legs
spread wide to display her furred snatch through which
her little pink nether lips grinned at him with faint mock-
ing. "That man sounds absolutely *dangerous*!"

As Thunder Brodie continued to rumble like a slow-
moving storm, his boots beginning to thud on the hotel's

carpeted steps, Longarm buckled his cartridge belt and holstered, double-action Frontier model Colt .44-40 around his waist, the soft leather sheath sitting snug and in the cross-draw position on his left hip, over his balbriggans. "Not to worry, Miss Nancy. This should just take a minute. Old Thunder sounds totally out of his mind. He was probably so happy to find himself alive after that tumble into the canyon, he's been whoring and drinking for the past five, six days straight."

The whole building shuddered as boots thumped and spurs chinged on the distant stairs.

Longarm donned his hat and glanced at the girl, who was just now slowly drawing her knees together. "Sit tight, now, hear? Whatever you do, Miss Nancy, you stay away from this door."

"Longarm!" Thunder Brodie's shout rose from down the hall—he was likely at the top of the stairs now. "Get on out here, you brush-faced scalawag! This dead man's come back, and he's gonna wear your oysters around his neck before the night is through!"

"Oh!" Nancy groaned, pulling the bed covers up over her pretty head and curling up in a tight ball.

Longarm turned the key in the lock, opened the door a crack, and peeked out. About fifty yards to his left down the broad hall carpeted in a deep, wine-red plush, and lit by guttering gas lamps, a stocky, bowlegged gent with long, greasy hair tumbling down from a heavy bandage wrapped around his head, and holding a bottle by its neck, bolted toward Longarm, yelling, "I know you're up here somewhere, you dirty dog!"

With that, Thunder Brodie lurched toward the hall's right side, raising his booted foot high, then slamming it against a door. The door burst inward with a loud, crunching bang, and Brodie filled the doorway with his broad, beefy frame—bottle in one hand, long-barreled Colt in the other.

"Longarm, you in here, you cowardly bastard?"

A woman's shrill scream rose from the room, as well a man's indignant bellow. Laughing, Brodie swung around and, gripping both the bottle and the cocked revolver, staggered to the other side of the hall. "Longarm, get out here, goddamnit! I'll kick in every fuckin' door in this whole consarned flophouse till I find the one you're in, ya yalla son of a bitch!"

With that, he kicked in another door and was met by a deep-throated curse. "Whoops, I reckon that ain't the right room, neither!" the old killer shouted in bellicose delight. As he started to turn away from the room, heading for another, Longarm slipped back into the room he was sharing with Miss Nancy, softly latching the door. He could walk on out and draw down on Brodie, but he'd be risking a lead swap with the drunken killer, and with the hotel being nearly full on account of the large beef buyer's convention, some innocent bystander might get pinked through one of the finely appointed but cheaply built hotel's thin walls.

He looked around, his cinnamon brows bunched with thought. Crossing the room, he quickly opened the door that led out to the balcony overlooking Buchanan Street.

From under the bedcovers, Nancy said in a quaking voice, "Marshal Long . . . ?"

"Shhh," Longarm said as Thunder Brodie kicked in another door down the hall. "You stay there and keep quiet as a church mouse, Miss Nancy. Don't show you're pretty little head till I tell ya it's safe."

The girl hunkered lower beneath the blankets and quilts, and Longarm went out onto the narrow, wrought-iron-railed, second-story balcony and closed the door softly behind him. It was after ten, but Amarillo was still hopping this Friday night, with suited beef buyers and their handlers as well as ranchers and saddle tramps strolling here and there and milling in front of the town's half dozen saloons, beer mugs or shot glasses in their fists.

Laughter of both men and women rose, as did the strains of guitars, pianos, and mandolins. From down near the railroad tracks, well-traveled, disgruntled cattle brayed in their holding pens, awaiting sale and shipment to Chicago, St. Louis, and other sundry points east.

The street was so loud with boisterous frolic, in fact, that out here on the balcony, Longarm could just barely hear Thunder Brodie's thunderous yells and the crunching bang of his kicked-in doors.

Walking softly but quickly on the balls of his feet, Longarm hurried about thirty feet down along the balcony and tried a room door. Locked. He hurried down to the next door, turned the knob. The latch clicked and the door opened outward.

Longarm stepped inside the room that was lit with a couple of bracket lamps and a candle on a cluttered dresser. He paused just inside the door, getting his bearings, vaguely noting that the room was laid out pretty much the way his own was. Swinging his head to the right, he grimaced.

On the large, canopied bed, a plump, naked girl with

her dark red hair in a bun straddled some gent whom Longarm could only see the pale, skinny legs of, poking out from the naked girl's broad, fleshy ass. With her back to Longarm, the girl—likely a whore servicing one of the middle-aged beef buyers from points east and enjoying a reprieve from wife and children—bounced wildly up and down on her haunches, sighing and groaning and making the bed bounce like a spindly boat on choppy seas.

Beneath her overly dramatic carrying-on, the dude said loudly, "Oh! Oh! Oh, yeah, that's it! Oh, Lord Jesus, please forgive me!"

And then he went back and started the monologue over again as the girl hunkered over him, trying for all she was worth, it appeared, to bring the strained coupling to fruition.

From out in the hall, Thunder Brodie's enraged voice rose, muffled with distance and obscured by the frolickers atop the nearby bed: "Goddamnit, Longarm! Quit cowerin' under your bed, and come out here and get the whuppin' and guttin' you deserve, you *murderin' son of a bitch*!"

Longarm crossed the room quickly. Fortunately, the two on the bed were too busy to notice the stranger in their midst, clad in balbriggans, boots, hat, and gun belt, and Longarm managed to slip silently into the hall, drawing the door carefully closed behind him and peering back toward his own room. Brodie was about four doors away from the room in which the banker's daughter cowered in Longarm's bed. The drunken outlaw was methodically if clumsily kicking in each door along his way.

Several half-dressed hotel guests—Easterners, by their

walleyed, horrifed gazes—stood in their open doorways, scowling after the drunken brigand and scratching their heads. When Brodie had finished kicking in one more door and continued staggering up the hall, his broad back to Longarm, the federal badge toter hoofed it forward, one hand on his pistol butt. Crossing the top of the broad stairs, he saw two beefy gents in too-tight suits climbing toward him, both wielding bung starters and severe looks on their lantern-jawed faces.

Hotel bouncers, they were. Likely sent by the manager to put down the unheeled dog tearing up his second floor.

Longarm waved the men off. As they stopped midway up the stairs, holding their clubs in both hands and running their skeptical gazes up and down Longarm's ridiculously garbed frame, Longarm continued tramping forward along the hall. He was within ten feet of the regaling outlaw and closing fast, his heart thudding anxiously.

Bam! went another smashed door.

"Longarm—you in here, you bastard?"

"Nope," Longarm said mildly. "I'm right behind you, Thunder, you rabid dog of a cat-lived son of a bitch."

Chapter 2

Standing roughly three feet in front of Longarm, just inside the room whose door he'd just kicked in, Thunder Brodie froze.

Or he tried to freeze. Pie-eyed from much hooch and smelling like a still, he sort of wobbled from foot to foot, his broad shoulders shifting like a teeter-totter. He turned his head slightly to one side, rolling a red-veined eye back toward Longarm. The bloodstained white bandage wrapped around the top of his head came down to just above his brows. His nose was swollen, and his face was marked with an assortment of scrapes and bruises.

In front of the outlaw, an old gray-haired man in a night sock and wash-worn balbriggans and an old woman in a shabby striped sleeping gown cowered together against the room's far wall, the old man halfheartedly holding an old-model Colt in his bony fist. The couple had likely traveled to Amarillo from out on the panhandle to sell beef and, having earned a small wad, decided to splurge on a nice hotel room only to have the raging, notorious rustler and bank robber Thunder Brodie tear their door down and wave a cocked Colt in their faces.

Longarm pressed his own Colt against Brodie's back. "Ease that hammer down and turn around slow. How dare you interrupt these fine folks' sleep."

"Yeah," the old woman croaked. "How dare you—"

She stopped when Brodie wheeled toward Longarm, swinging his gun around. Longarm thrust his left hand forward, to grab the killer's wrist while raising his own pistol and slamming it hard against the side of Thunder Brodie's stout, bandaged skull.

"Oh!" Brodie grunted, making an agonized expression and dropping his bottle.

At the same time, Longarm closed his left hand over the top of Brodie's gun, the barrel of which was shoved into his side, just above his cartridge belt, and felt the hammer bite the webbed flesh between his thumb and index finger.

He knew a harrowing moment as he looked down to see the barrel pressed against his lower left belly, into which it would have delivered a .45-caliber pill had Longarm's hand not slipped between the hammer and the firing pin a sixteenth of a second before the deadly detonation. As Brodie dropped to his knees, giving another sigh, Longarm pulled the killer's pistol out of his withering grip and stepped back.

Brodie sagged against the doorframe, eyelids fluttering. Stretching his lips back from his cracked, yellow teeth, he lifted a hand toward his bandaged head. His arm dropped as if it were broken, and Brodie collapsed.

"Serves him right!" the old woman chirped. "Hit him

again. Nearly gave both me and old Homer here heart strokes!"

Longarm holstered his own Colt, then pried the hammer of Brodie's gun back, to release his hand.

"Feel the flames of hell warmin' your feet, do you, Longarm?"

The federal badge toter looked up to see the two bouncers stuffed into undersized suits standing in the hall before him, with a dozen or so sleepy-eyed, anxious faces peering out of open doors behind and around them. Longarm had been in town a couple of days, waiting to hop the next train to Denver, and he'd gotten to know the bouncers and bartenders and a few of the pleasure girls from the Palo Duro Inn's saloon. The clean-shaven fellow who'd spoken was Fitzsimmons, while his walrus-mustached companion was Ingram. They looked so much alike, with similar-sized muscles bulging here and there, their trunklike necks threatening to split their paper collars, that they could have been brothers though Longarm knew they weren't.

"Reckon I did hear one of Ole Scratch's hounds yip," Longarm said, feeling the giddiness of the close call dancing in his head and swimming in his vision. He stuffed Brodie's revolver behind his cartridge belt, then removed the big bowie from the killer's belt sheath. He gave the knife to one of the bouncers, then stooped down to pull the killer's voluminous bulk over his right shoulder.

"Give me a hand here, fellas."

Both bouncers stepped forward to help Longarm hoist Brodie's smelly two hundred pounds, until the killer's head was hanging down Longarm's back. "Now, then," Longarm said, nodding at the old couple still regarding him and his unconscious prisoner with wary fascination and not a little condemnation, "let's move on out of here and let these good folks go back to sleep."

"Harumph!" the old woman said.

The old man staggered forward in his stockinged feet, chuckling. "You sure stuffed his pipe for him, I'll give ya that, whoever ya are."

"Second time, too. Hope this time it's for good."

Longarm gave a parting wink to the old gent and started off down the hall toward the stairs, staggering under the big killer's deadweight.

"You want us to haul that devil over to the sheriff's office, Longarm?" Ingram asked. "You don't look like you're exactly dressed fer the street."

"You're right, I ain't. But I'm gonna haul this asshole over to the hoosegow my ownself. I'll never sleep till I see him behind lock and key." Longarm turned at the top of the stairs, not completely inadvertently smacking the comatose Brodie's head against the oak newel post with a dull thwack. "And I reckon tonight won't be the first night the good folks of Amarillo will witness a man makin' a fool of himself in public. This is Texas, ain't it?"

Longarm chuckled and, leaving the two bouncers standing there looking incredulous, started down the broad, carpeted stairs. At the bottom and during his stroll across the saloon, he received a hearty round of applause from the inebriated beef buyers and sellers, and several catcalls from the drunkest of the reveling men as well as a few of the sporting girls decked out in their finest and skimpiest.

A bartender, whose name was Saul Hightower, and

who had set up Longarm with more than a few of the lawman's preferred Maryland ryes and thick dark ales over the past couple of days, shouted above the din: "Damn, Custis, I thought you'd killed that son of a bitch and left him to the bobcats!"

Longarm removed one hand from his deadweight parcel to flip the stout and immaculately coifed and tailored barman a timeless gesture of bawdy reproof, to which Hightower responded with rumbling guffaws. The din followed Longarm out the batwings, across the crowded gallery, and into the broad, rutted street, which he traversed at an angle, heading for the sheriff's office housed in a humble, nondescript clapboard building connected by a dogtrot to the Potter County Courthouse.

He mounted the narrow stoop that, like the rest of the building, was suspended a foot above the ground by stone pilings to prevent tunneling under the cellblock. The gilt-lettered front window was lit, and behind drawn red curtains Longarm could see the sheriff sitting at his desk, working by lantern light.

Longarm swung around to use Thunder Brodie's bloody-bandaged head to knock on the office door. He watched the sheriff, Bill Rackman, push heavily up from his desk and tramp to the door with a thump of boots and a rattle of large-roweled Texas spurs.

"Longarm, what in the hell . . . ?" Rackman said, running his eyes down the federal lawman's unprofessionally clad frame, then at the comatose gent hanging like an abnormally large grain sack over his left shoulder.

Grunting against Brodie's considerable weight and the intensifying ache in his shoulder, Longarm said, "It's Thunder Brodie, Bill. Turns out I didn't leave him in that canyon, after all. Hope you got an empty cell for the son of a bitch."

"I thought you done killed him!"

"Step aside, Bill." Longarm bulled his way into the sheriff's office, making a beeline for the cellblock door at the room's rear. "And open that door before the big bastard dislocates my shoulder!"

The sheriff of Potter County grabbed a key ring off a ceiling joist and hustled over to the cellblock door flanked by two gun racks and a map of northern Texas on the office's back wall. Riffling through the keys, Rackman tossed a wing of silver-gray hair from his right eye and frowned again at the load on Longarm's shoulder. "Well, where the hell'd you find him?"

"I didn't find him," Longarm grunted. "He found me."

As Rackman pulled the heavy cellblock door open, stepping back out of Longarm's way, the federal badge toter stomped into the cellblock, making a beeline for one of two empty cells at the block's rear. The other four cages were occupied mostly by snoring drunks though one held two men in ratty trail garb sporting bloody knuckles and swollen eyes, one with a white bandage over a nose ballooned to the size of a small, clenched fist.

Both saddle tramps watched Longarm and Rackman dully through the bars of their cell as the sheriff rushed to open the door of the empty cell on the right side of the corridor. Longarm followed at a shambling gait, leaning toward the side of his burden, his low-heeled cavalry boots clacking on the heavy flagstones. Rackman swung the heavy, barred door open with a tooth-gnashing screech of dry hinges, and Longarm crabbed inside, his knees giving beneath him, then turned his back on the cell's single cot, and heaved up on Brodie's legs.

The heavy killer tumbled down Longarm's back to land upon the cot with a heavy thump and a groan.

Longarm stepped away from the cot, rubbing his sore shoulder and sucking air through his teeth. "Holy Christ, that son of a bitch is heavy!"

"Damn deadly, too. How is it he came lookin' for you, though, Custis, when he was supposed to be dead in that canyon?"

Longarm leaned over the cot to give the slumbering Brodie a good frisking. He'd take no more chances on the man. In fact, he wouldn't rest easy until the circuit judge had the old border bandit dangling from a hangman's noose, which would likely be sooner rather later, given the killer's fierce history and the fact that he'd murdered two Texas Rangers who'd led up the posse that had initially tracked Brodie's gang across the Brazos River.

Ambushed them, hacked them up with bowie knives, and hanged them.

"Obviously, he wasn't dead," Longarm said, pulling Brodie's right boot off and looking inside, making a face at the smell. "Though he sure as hell *looked* dead from the ridge above the canyon. So dead, in fact, I saw no reason to risk life and limb pulling him out of that chasm just so I could haul his dead carcass back to Amarillo for a nice church funeral."

Rackman watched Longarm remove Brodie's other boot, from which a black-handled stiletto tumbled onto the floor. "I'm with you that far."

Longarm removed a small pocket pistol from a sheath strapped to the killer's left calf, then stooped to retrieve the knife from the floor. "Well, he wasn't dead. Obviously. And I reckon after a few days of whoring and getting some doctoring in one of them little Mex villages around Black Mesa, he got him a horse and headed north with one hell of a chip on his shoulder, hunting the lawdog that turned his gang toe down . . . except for ole Brodie himself."

Longarm gave the outlaw, who grunted and fluttered his eyelids painfully, another careful inspection. Then he stepped back out of the cell, and Rackman closed the door. "Imagine the gall of that bastard . . . trackin' you back here to the scene of his deadly crime."

Longarm stared bemusedly through the iron bars at the snarling, semiconscious outlaw. "Seems like a lot of work just to make a loud-assed drunken fool of himself, kicking in doors over at the Palo Duro Inn and bellowing at the top of his damn lungs."

"Whiskey!" Brodie wheezed, suddenly lifting his head from the cot and pressing both his big hands to his face. "Oh, Lordy, please—*whiskey!*"

"You've had enough whiskey, Brodie," Longarm said. "Time to sober up for the hangman."

Brodie blinked. Blood was dribbling down from beneath his bandage to run in a single streak down over his ear. "Please," he begged, sitting up and grinding the heels of his hands into his temples. "Oh, please . . . I'm sorry fer my sins. Just please give me some whiskey. I 'bout broke my head clear open when I hit the floor of that canyon. Had to guzzle panther juice just to keep from goin' plain loco with misery. Now, after you laid me out with your pistol, Longarm, you son of a bitch . . . Why the hell didn't you just shoot me?"

"And cheat the hangman?"

Sheriff Rackman chuckled. "They're always sorry once they're in there. Surprised to hear it from that wolf there, though." He glanced at Longarm. "Don't worry—I'll wire the circuit judge first thing in the mornin'. He'll be here on the next flier. I'll have the boys start settin' up the gallows. We'll hang him five minutes after the judge's gavel falls."

Longarm headed for the open cellblock door. "Don't turn your back on him, Bill."

As Longarm passed the cell in which the two battered saddle tramps stood, resting their wrists on the bars and staring at Brodie, who was sobbing and sighing in the shadows at the back of the cellblock, the tramp with the broken nose said, "So, that's Thunder Brodie."

"That's him, fellas." On Longarm's heels, Rackman gave his keys a couple of loud, contented jiggles. "But it won't be for long."

"Damn," said the other tramp dully. "I thought he'd be bigger."

"He's plenty big enough," Longarm said and tramped through the cellblock door.

In the main office, Longarm turned to Rackman, who was locking the heavy door, and opened his mouth to speak.

The sheriff cut him off. "One step ahead o' ya, Custis. I'll have a deputy watching Brodie every second till we hang his infernal carcass. You go on back over to the Palo Duro and crawl into bed." He chuckled as he raked his gaze over the federal's ridiculously garbed frame. "That does appear the place you best belong."

Longarm looked around. "I've got all the confidence

in the world, Bill, but . . . uh . . . where's your deputies?"

"Louie and Craig are out patrolin' the saloons, tryin' to keep that crowd o' out-of-towners on their leashes. The other two, Driscoll and Caldwell, got called over to the banker's place."

"Plaza?"

Rackman nodded as he tossed his keys on his desk and pulled his duck pants up his broad hips. "Seems the banker's daughter, Miss Nancy, turned up missing. Oh, I'm sure she's around. Probably over to the west side of the railroad tracks. That's where we've done found her before."

Longarm's cheeks were instantly as hot as an iron skillet. In all the commotion with Brodie, he'd forgotten he'd left the banker's daughter in his bed at the inn, cowering under the blankets. Rackman mistook the federal's blushing scowl for curiosity.

"Oh, the girl looks like butter wouldn't melt in her mouth," the sheriff said, absently running a thick, brown figure along a scar on his jaw. "But I got me a feelin' iron would turn to pudding on the tip o' that tongue o' hers. I reckon her daddy might keep her on too tight a rein, 'cause when she busts out of the barn, she runs a long ways, if'n you get my drift." He winked and sagged into the swivel chair behind his desk. "A little embarrassing for the Plazas, I'd imagine—havin' their fifteen-year-old daughter prancin' like a mare in heat around the Mex side o' town!"

"Fifteen?" Longarm scowled, flushing deeper. "I thought she was seventeen!"

Chapter 3

Rackman looked up at Longarm from his desk chair, beetling his silver-gray brows. He cocked his head to one side and narrowed an eye. "You haven't seen our randy Miss Plaza, now, have you, Custis?"

"Of course, I haven't seen her!" Longarm chuckled, but it sounded even to him like he was choking. "I just remembered her tellin' me in the Plaza parlor she was seventeen, that's all."

"Don't doubt it a bit." Rackman chuckled. "Why, she was likely after you, ya damn fool. Probably heard about what a ladies' man ya are, and wanted to know from first-hand experience what all the fuss was about."

Rackman laughed. "Stay away, lessen you want a ring-tail under your covers and her old man's shotgun up your ass!"

"Good advice," Longarm rasped, feeling the muscles of his hot face draw taut as he made his way to the jail office's front door. He suddenly couldn't get out of there fast enough. "Damn good advice. If I do just happen to

see the girl on my way back to the Palo Duro, I'll send
her right on home."

"You do that. And I'll put a deputy outside Brodie's
cell just as soon as we find that hot-blooded Plaza girl."

"You do that. I'll check on him in the mornin', before
I hop the train back for Denver."

"Sleep tight, Longarm! Might want think twice next
time about walkin' around town in your underwear! Ha!"

The sheriff's self-satisfied laughter was muffled by the
door that Longarm closed behind him. Stepping off the
gallery, he headed directly across the street, attracting
more than a little attention from the howling drunks on
the boardwalks fronting the saloons and cantinas.

Rather than enduring another round of catcalls at the
Palo Duro Inn, however, he walked around behind the
place and tramped up the back outside stairs. A young
whore and her jake were in the throes of carnal passion
near the bottom of the steps. A quick glance told Longarm the man, clad in a cheap checked suit and bowler
hat, had the sporting girl bent forward over a rain barrel,
her pink skirt thrown up over her pale, slender back. He
and the sporting lass were far too busy, grunting and
groaning and splashing water, to worry about how Longarm was dressed, so he managed to climb the stairs in
peace and enter the second-floor hallway undetected.

Except for several slumberous snores, all was quiet in
the wake of Thunder Brodie's thunderous assault. All
the damaged doors were closed, likely held there by
chairs wedged beneath knobs.

Longarm tried his own door. Still locked. His key was
inside. Cheeks still burning from the knowledge he'd
gained about the Plaza girl—as a rule, he never fucked

females under the age of sixteen, and even then the sixteen-year-old had to be one mighty clean and friendly Mexican whore—he cleared his throat impatiently and tapped his knuckles against his own door panel.

Silence.

Had the girl left? That would have been fine and dandy, because he meant to get rid of her, anyway. Diddling a seventeen-year-old daughter of a banker was one thing, but cavorting with a fifteen-year-old was damn near depravity. He cursed his growing bad luck. His room key was on the other side of the door lock!

He tapped again.

A girl's thin, cautious voice said, "Who is it?"

"Longarm." He looked around anxiously, making sure no one else was in the hall, then said just loudly enough to be heard on the other side of the door, "Open up, Miss Nancy, my sweet."

He heard the bedsprings sigh. Bare feet padded across the floor, and a shadow moved under the door. The key rattled in the lock, and then the door pulled slightly black and the girl's cornflower blue eyes stared at him through the crack. A foot beneath the eye was a tender pink nipple.

The girl's lips lifted a relieved smile, and she pulled the door open and stepped back . . . naked as the day she was born but a whole lot more grown up. There wasn't a stitch on her little, voluptuous figure. Not even a piece of jewelry. Her rich blond hair was piled loosely atop her head. She cupped her full, tender breasts in her hands and set one foot atop the other, wagging a knee and arching her brows as she looked up at him with those innocent eyes.

"Did you throw the varmint in jail, Marshal Long?"

Longarm glanced once more into the hall, then quickly, quietly closed the door. He turned to the girl, who remained standing before him, cupping her breasts, pooching out her lips, and wagging her knee. He swallowed down the knot in his throat and ignored the pull in his groin.

"Yes, Miss Nancy—the varmint is hauled off to the hoosegow to await his dance with Ole Scratch."

"Who?"

"Never mind." Longarm doffed his hat and removed his cartridge belt. "What I'd like for you to do now is leave here pronto. Get dressed and skedaddle, go on back home to dear old Dad and dear old Ma, and forget this night ever happened . . . and thank God it hadn't gone any further than it did. I guess I really should thank old Thunder Brodie for making it out of that canyon alive to save me from my own damn self!"

He went to the dresser and splashed Maryland rye into a water glass, took one more look at the girl's naked figure, felt his heart twist painfully, and threw the liquor straight back.

"What on earth are you talking about, Marshal Long?" Miss Nancy's peaches-and-cream cheeks pinkened with chagrin. "You want me to leave? But it's so early and"— her face blossoming with one of her rich, beguiling smiles, she strode toward him, lifting her arms toward his neck—"and . . . I'm so . . . *naaaked.*"

"You are at that, but not for long." Longarm picked her dress and underfrillies off the floor and shoved them at her, covering her breasts. "Get yourself dressed and run along, girl. You told me you were seventeen, but I learned over at the jailhouse—where I also learned that two deputies are out scouring the town for you—that you're only fifteen. Now, you might wonder how two years can make a difference, but it does." Longarm was trying to keep his eyes off the girl's sexy little body as well as her sadly pooched lips. "I'm not one to frolic with children. Especially not a child of a prominent family such as yours. So . . . damnit, Miss Nancy, will you please stop standing there staring up at me like I just gutted your favorite teddy bear and get dressed? You need to run along like a good little girl!"

She shuffled around in front of him, wrapped her arms around his neck, and rose up on her little pudgy toes to plant a delicate, wet kiss on his lips. "You don't really want me to go, Marshal Long."

"I most certainly do, Miss Nancy."

"No, you don't." She kissed him again, and he tipped his head back away from her. "Know how I know?"

Longarm scowled at the girl staring up at him, her nose about three inches away from his chin.

Suddenly, she lowered her hands. With a heady thrill that nearly buckled his knees, he felt her small, soft, warm hands wrap around his cock, which, he looked down to see, had sprung free of the button fly of his long-handle bottoms. The fully engorged and jutting shaft was grinding its large, purple head against the girl's pleasantly plump belly.

She'd grabbed it with both hands, one high, one low, and looked up at him coyly. Slowly bending her knees, she dropped down in front of him, lowering her head but keeping her eyes on his as she squeezed and pumped him gently with her hands.

"No, no," Longarm heard himself grunt, just loudly enough to be heard above his heart's hammering in his ears. "Now, see here now, Miss Nancy, this is the very thing I've been trying to avoid."

He reached for her arms, to pull her back up, but she'd dropped down out of his reach, and he couldn't get his own knees to bend . . . not with the girl's soft, warm hands on his fully engorged organ, he couldn't.

If he tried, he might fall and never get up again.

When Miss Nancy's knees hit the floor, she smiled up at him, her blue eyes flashing devilishly.

"Sure you want me to stop, Marshal Long?"

She was pure evil, this girl. Pure, raw, sugarcoated evil.

"Ah . . . hell . . ." Longarm sighed.

"I didn't think you would. I may be only fifteen, but I've sucked on these here things before." Miss Nancy gave Longarm's cock a little wag and touched her tongue to the end of it. "Maybe not one as fully grown as yours— my God, you're hung like the horses in my daddy's stable!—but I'm just gonna think of it like a big old nickel sucker I bought at Mr. Wilson's candy shop. You let me know if I'm going about it the right way, okay?"

She looked up at him. A little thread of saliva wavered between her wet, bottom lip and the tip of Longarm's cock.

Longarm only cursed.

The girl giggled, then closed her mouth down over the mushroom head of his shaft, going straight to work groaning and making loud sucking sounds and nearly causing Longarm's heart to stop when she'd taken him so deep that her lips nearly touched his scrotum.

Longarm felt no guilt over the blow job he received from Miss Nancy Plaza.

Whatever the girl's age in years, she was nearly as old as Longarm in experience, and what she hadn't experienced physically, the naughty daughter of George Plaza had certainly fantasized about.

No, he felt no guilt about the blow job. Nor about the mad fucking that had followed that intoxicating, beguiling bit of fellatio. He'd hammered the girl so hard while shouldering her knees up and back against her jaws that he thought the bed would fall through the floor into the saloon hall below.

And still, after going at it like back-alley curs over and over again, she was reluctant to leave the lawman's room and only did so after Longarm professed that he was not only done fucking her but any other girl he ran into for the next three months, so strained was his heart, so chased was his dong.

He thought he might have even pulled a couple of muscles in his legs while ramming his piston into the girl's hot, sopping, insatiable depths.

But he had to admit even a week later, as he ran up the marble steps of the Federal Building near the U.S. Mint in downtown Denver, that, all in all, despite Thunder Brodie's interruption, his time with Miss Nancy had been rare and bewitching, right up with one of his best nights ever. One that he'd remember for a long, long time. He might even take the memory with him into his next life, if other lives were indeed possible and not just

the hokum of a girl he'd once known—some saloon girl
from Boulder by way of Georgia who called herself a
Buddhist and a disciple of Tibetan monks, though she
seemed a tad on the jealous side, mighty quick to anger,
could down a bottle of cheap wine in under an hour, and
curse everyone in sight with the rage of a drunken Irish
gandy dancer.

"Hidy-ho, Henry," Longarm greeted the immaculately garbed and coifed sissy who played the typewriter
in his boss's outer office. "How the hell's it hangin' this
bright, crisp Monday mornin'? Get any over the week-
end or you too busy rubbin' Webley's Foot Cream into
your old ma's bunions?"

The kid, whose name was Henry but whose last name
had never stuck in Longarm's memory, stopped playing
his typewriter long enough to sniff. "Marshal Vail is
waiting for you, Deputy Long. You may go right in. I'll
have your travel vouchers ready in a few minutes."

With that, he thumbed his round spectacles up his
fine, pale nose splashed with ever so faint freckles and
resumed hammering the keys of the loud, ugly contrap-
tion with the finesse of one of the overly civilized piano
players that Miss Cynthia Larimer was always making the
lawman endure at the finer venues around Denver.

Longarm tossed his half-smoked nickel cheroot into
the cuspidor by one of the Windsor waiting chairs lining
the back wall. "Nice chattin' with ya, Henry." He knocked
on frosted glass door on Henry's far side, in the room's
left wall, and in which MARSHAL WILLIAM VAIL, 1ST
DISTRICT COURT had been etched in now-faded gold-leaf
lettering. "Hope we can do it again real soon."

At the same time that Billy Vail bellowed, "Get in

here, Longarm!" the federal badge toter pushed through the door and doffed his snuff brown, flat-brimmed hat, blinking against the rich cloud of aromatic cigar smoke wafting throughout the room like a ground fog on a warm mountain morning after a chill night in the spring-time. The fog was so thick, in fact, that the huge desk sitting the middle of the cluttered, shelf-lined room, and the pudgy little man sitting dwarfed behind it, were mere blurs inside it.

"Jesus Christ, Chief!" Longarm waved his hand in front of his face. "You really oughta cut down on them things."

"On what things?"

Blinking against the sting in his eyes, Longarm an-gled the red Moroccan leather guest chair in front of his boss's massive desk piled high with sheaves of paper and manila file folders bleeding travel vouchers and re-ports turned in by other deputies. "Them things like the one you got in your hand. You know—big as a German blood sausage and spewing smoke from the front end, kind of soggy on the other."

Chief Marshal Billy Vail, who at one time had been a sight to behold on horseback and armed with six-guns, now looked more like an overfed accountant relegated to the dingy back room of some shipping warehouse. He was pudgy, pale, and bespectacled, with thinning, sandy-gray hair angling back from a sharp widow's peak. He wore a rumpled white shirt under a gravy-stained wool vest, his sleeves rolled up his pasty arms. He looked at the cigar in the hand he had resting against his right cheek and frowned.

"Oh—you mean my stogies. General Larimer sent

me over a fresh box the other day. Damn good Cuban cigars in appreciation for services rendered at the Fourth of July Parade—you know, the one you spent under the grandstand boning the general's comely niece while the United States Cavalry and Infantry Corps showed off their wares to several thousand cheering patriots?"

"Oh, that parade."

"Yeah, the one in which the marshal's office was supposedly acting as bodyguards to the good general and his family, including Miss Cynthia, who likely spent most of that time—in which you were being paid from government coffers—with your cock in her mouth."

Longarm winced, pinched his thighs together. Just the mention of fellatio reminded him of the severe chafing he'd received just last week from Missy Nancy Plaza. "All right, Chief, never mind, never mind. Let's hop away from your unhealthy and sedentary office habits to my next assignment, shall we?"

Chapter 4

Chief Marshal Billy Vail took a long drag from the thick stogie in his hand, then, blowing more smoke into the already heavy cloud that had nearly rendered him and his desk invisible to the tall, dark-haired, mustachioed deputy sitting across from him, said, "Next assignment. Right. Well, we got trouble at a little mining village up high in the Rockies. A place called Sully Creek, straight west of here and nestled in a little canyon between Jim Peak and Bear Ridge, just on the other side of the Divide. Helluva place, all but unreachable from the end of September until about mid-May, though I hear there ain't too much snow up there yet. At least, not enough to restrict train travel."

"I've heard of it. Believe I might have even spent the night up there. Nosebleed country. Only the heartiest of the gold panners and silver diggers, and the meanest of the whores, last more than a few weeks. What kind of trouble?" Again, Longarm waved his hand in front of his face, in a futile attempt to clear the air and find some oxygen, and sank back in the upholstered leather guest

chair. "I'd think a place like that would be quieting down
this time of year. And, if I may be so bold, Chief, anyone
who heads up that gall-blasted high in the mountains
this time of year—pret' near the end of the first week in
October—might not be seen or heard from again until
the lilacs are once more blooming along the banks of
Cherry Creek."

"As the nun told the priest with a penchant for spirits
and fallen women—tough titty. That's where you're heading just as soon as Henry's done typing up your travel
vouchers and the next narrow gauge crawls in from Ever-
green. The village constable and the constable's deputy
were murdered up there last week. The mayor sent a
telegram asking for help finding the killers and placing a
new badge toter." Vail plucked a tobacco flake from his
tongue and flicked it in the general direction of his waste-
basket. "The request by a local official for help in the
matter of two dead local lawmen can't very well be de-
nied, now, can it? Or postponed until spring."

"Ah, shit," Longarm grunted, turning his hat on his
knee. "So you want me to go up there and try to find the
killer or killers and pin a badge on a marginally qualified
local. And I'm supposed to do all this before Sully
Creek is buried under eight feet of snow."

"Shouldn't be hard. Most likely whoever killed them
lawmen is a known enemy of theirs. There may even
have been witnesses. Search me. The mayor's cable was
pretty short and to the point—not much more than 'Constable, deputy constable dead. Stop. Send help. Stop.'
For all I know, the killers are known, but there's no one
around to take them into custody. My guess is it's some

rowdy drunk who lives up there and likely goes ape shit when the snow clouds start rolling across the Divide.

"So your main job will likely be getting another lawman seated. Sully Creek is small but maintains a population of fifteen or twenty over the winter—mostly bachelor miners who can get pretty out of control when they're not working, which they can't do in the snow. The place is gonna need at least an obligatory badge stumbling around to keep those miners on some semblance of a leash, or they'll end up killing each other with shovels and terrorizing what few women and children stay up there through the winter, maybe burning the whole damn place to the ground."

"Shouldn't be a town up that high, anyway, Chief."

"Well, there is. And that's where you're headed. So, stop wasting my time sitting there with a chip on your shoulder—believe me, after all these years, I do know how you feel about cold-weather assignments—and hustle on down to Union Station. Do not, and I repeat *do not* take the time for a quickie with Miss Larimer. The narrow gauge should be here soon. And don't forget to snag your travels docs from Henry."

"Miss Cynthia ain't in town, Chief." Long-faced, Longarm rose heavily and set his hat on his head. He could already feel the chill at those high-altitude climes deep in his bones, see the snow hanging heavy on the fir trees, the smoke gushing from the tin chimney pipes of the prospectors' humble shacks. "She's down in Mexico, way down south where it's nice and warm, drawing pictures of jungle Injuns and such."

"Glad to hear it. The general would be, too, if he

didn't believe your cock-and-bull about you and her having only a 'professional' relationship."

Guffawing, the chief marshal sat back in his high-backed leather chair and, with a smug, self-satisfied expression, took a deep drag on his stogie. His eyes glinted devilishly behind his spectacles as his face nearly disappeared behind a cloud of fresh smoke the color of old burlap. "If he knew you were fuckin' that well-schooled little heiress seven ways from Sunday, mounting her like a goddamn Russian racehorse with the springtime craze, the old boy'd likely get out one of them big bird guns of his made in Sweden or Prussia or wherever the fuck he gets 'em and fill your ass with a few loads of well-deserved buckshot."

"If I was headin' down to where she is right now, running around half naked with the natives, that buckshot would be a small price to pay, Billy."

"Yeah, well, you're not—you're heading for winter, Custis. Enjoy yourself!" More laughter emanated from the heavy white cloud that was Billy Vail and his all-but-invisible desk. "And I suggest you keep it in your pants while you're there. I hear the Sully Creek whores are not only the ugliest but the deadliest in the central Rockies, with more than one poor old miner running down from them climes with such a bad case of the pony drip that the screams are said to be louder than the wind up in them snowy rocks!"

Blinking against the smoke in his eyes, Longarm went out and shut the door quickly behind him, hearing Billy's laughter dwindle very gradually to rumbling, self-congratulatory chuckles. "I don't think it's nice—his revelin' in my misery."

The coifed and tailored sissy snorted, sniffed, and shoved a folder across his desk. "Your vouchers, Deputy Long. Please try to keep things in order, and do please try to write your reports in a legible hand this time."

Grumbling, Longarm crossed the room and went out.

"Hey, bubby, how 'bout one of them rags you're hawkin'?" Longarm hailed the *Rocky Mountain News* boy in the bustling Union Station. He knew the kid—who couldn't have been a day over ten, if that—from his multiple comings and goings to and from the West's busiest train hub and figured he was one of the towheaded younker's most regular customers.

"You got it, Longarm!" The soiled and ragged urchin with a winning smile in spite of two chipped front teeth and a cracked lip no doubt incurred from street brawls with competing news hawks, handed over the latest edition of Denver's newspaper and held out his hand for Longarm's proferred nickel, which included the price of the paper as well as a four-and-a-half-cent tip. "Where you headin' now? Off to shoot some bad men, maybe invite 'em to necktie parties held in their honor?"

The boy's loud, hearty laugh echoed off the vast station's sandstone walls and high, arched ceiling, echoing above the din of a thousand striding travelers, and Longarm wondered vaguely and fleetingly if the child had been fathered by his own self-satisfied boss, Billy Vail.

"Now, bubby," Longarm said reprovingly, rolling an unlit cheroot from one corner of his mouth to the other as he scanned the paper's front page. "You know I never go out with the intention of shootin' anyone. Always gotta give 'em the opportunity to give up first. But if they

don't"—he grinned devilishly over the paper at the kid
and made a gun with his thumb and index finger—"bam!
Deader'n last year's Christmas goose."

The kid grinned largely, showing those chipped front
teeth, blue eyes flashing with vicarious delight. As Longarm turned away from the boy, who was being hailed
by a whiskey drummer sitting in a shoeshine chair, a
bearded, bull-chested hombre in a brown suit and bowler
hat plowed smack into him, knocking him sideways.

"Outta the way there, mister! Step aside! Step aside
for Miss Hathaway!"

Longarm scowled indignantly at the big gent, then
looked at the tight group on the big gent's heels—three
other big gents clustered around a queenly-looking redhead in a velvet green cape over an immaculately tailored gown trimmed with sequins. The redhead was decked
out in so much jewelry that the morning light angling
through the station's tall, arched windows and flashing
off her gold earrings and ruby necklaces made Longarm's eyes ache as though pierced by miniature javelins.
As the group barreled toward him, he could smell the
ripe cherry aroma of her obviously high-priced cologne,
see the flawless porcelain color of her long neck and
china-delicate ears and nose as well as the rich golden
brown of her sparkling eyes.

He took all this in within a second or two after his
collision with the first beefy gent, who'd knocked Longarm's newspaper out of his hands. As Longarm stooped
to grab the paper before it was trampled by the fast-
approaching cavalcade, another beefy gent shouldered
into him, sort of pushing him back and around and into
the path of the English queen or whomever the insouci-

antly beautiful creature was striding toward him with her delicately chiseled nose in the air.

The woman's eyes widened when they saw the big, tall, mustachioed gent stooped before her, and she gave a gasp as her eyes dropped to the double-action Frontier model Colt positioned for the cross draw on the lawman's left hip. She stopped suddenly, pale cheeks coloring, the beauty mark just left of her long, rich mouth turning a shade darker.

"Hey, hey, hey!" intoned the beefy gent striding beside the woman. He moved quickly forward, sort of skip-hopping in front of her and whipping a bulky arm out to shove the tall, newspaper-clutching plebian out of the queenly one's way.

Longarm held his ground, scowling and growling, "One of you boys shoves me again, I'm gonna break the arm he's shovin' with over my knee. I got as much right to this here piece of marble flooring as the queen bitch does, and since I was here first, you and her'll just have to take the trouble of walking around me"—he locked eyes with the beefy gent who had stopped his forearm within an inch of Longarm's chest—"unless he wants a .44 shoved up his ass and triggered into his liver."

The beefy gent he was glaring at glared back. The entire cavalcade had stopped in front of Longarm—aside from the first gent, who was scrambling back toward the group and mewling and yowling impatiently. As the gent in front of Longarm shoved his chin up toward Longarm's, the man's ruddy face turning dark with fury, the queen bitch standing behind him in all her queen-bee glory said in a tone of one speaking to an unhealed cur, "Louis, no!"

Louis continued to glare up at Longarm, his fist clenched so tightly that his knuckles had turned white, for another two or three seconds. Then he lowered his arm, decompressing his lips, and beckoned to the others behind him. They ushered the queen in a broad arc around Longarm, the queen bee in their midst turning her queenly head to regard the tall plebian with open disdain before letting her eyes rake him up and down quickly but not very subtly. As she hoofed it on toward the door facing the tracks, she wrinkled her nose, swiveled her regal head forward, and let her liege guide her out onto the loading platform, where the narrow-gauge mountain crawler was waiting in a steam bath threaded with sparking coal cinders.

Longarm went over and grabbed his gear—saddlebags, war bag, fleece-lined mackinaw, and Winchester '73—from the bench where he'd been sitting before spying the newspaper boy. As he settled the possibles on one shoulder and clutched his rifle in his other hand, he growled around the cigar in his teeth, "I just hope that uppity bitch ain't headin' where I'm headin'. If she is, me and her dogs are liable to lock canines."

Chapter 5

Hoping the snooty Miss Hathaway, whoever the hell she was, and her beefy bodyguards weren't heading the same direction Longarm was, nor sharing his ride, had been too much to hope for. Heading for one of the coaches of the five-car combination, which didn't include the diamond-stacked Shay locomotive nor tender car heaped with split wood, Longarm stopped suddenly.

He leaned away from the car he'd been approaching to peer back along the tracks, to where a bright pink car trimmed in brass and fancy yellow scrolling sat between the caboose and the parlor car. White, gild-edged shades were drawn over the windows that sat snug in shiny black frames, and each pane was monogrammed JH in delicate gold-leaf scroll. The door at the front of the car bore the same letters in its upper glass panel, whose pale, gold-laced curtains were closed to outside gawkers, and two brass lion lanterns snarled at each side. The brass railing enclosing the outside vestibule and three side steps was worked into all sorts of artistic shapes and figures.

If the obviously private car didn't belong to the high-falutin bitch who'd tried to mow him down in the station a few minutes ago, he'd walk to Sully Creek barefoot.

"At least she has her own car," he grumbled as he climbed aboard the coach car behind an old German woman with as an ass broad as a rain barrel.

He made his way along the cramped aisle, heading for the rear of the car, then tossed his saddlebags and war bag into the cramped overhead racks, reminded once again how much he hated the narrow-gauge mountain trains for their diminutive size and diminished legroom, not to mention the traditionally slow speeds. Making way for a couple of saddle tramps squeezing past him with saddles on their shoulders and quirleys smoldering between their lips, he sank into a seat with his back to a bulkhead. He'd had to parry enough assassination attempts by owlhoots whom he'd piss-burned one way or another to know that his broad back was a nice, big bull's-eye to a great many around the mostly lawless frontier.

He doubted, however, that anyone would take the trouble of climbing into the high, cold Rockies this time of the year just to feed him a pill he couldn't digest. People boarding this train had a damn good reason for doing so, and any would-be bushwhacker could wait until he was strolling in the Denver sunshine. On this mountain mini-train, he was more likely to get killed in an avalanche than by an assassin's bullet.

With a sigh, thinking about the contrast between his destination and Cynthia Larimer's current vacation spot, he leaned his rifle against the seat across from him, hiked a boot onto a knee, lit his cheroot, and opened his paper. He hoped no one would claim the three seats around him. Since Uncle Sam was too cheap to spring for a sleeper car, he liked to spread out as much as he could in these cramped environs, and that wasn't much.

He read the paper slowly, knowing he had plenty of time to kill, and watched the countryside pass by his window slowly. Even more slowly the pines and granite and sandstone escarpments slid past as the train crept up into the mountains straight west of Denver—so slowly, in fact, that when Longarm looked up from his paper a time or two, he thought they were standing still.

He read, slept, smoked, and a couple of times he strolled up and down the aisle of his own coach and that of the next one. Neither was very full or, thank God, pestered by screaming urchins or squawking livestock— chickens, water fowl, or even pigs—like that which country and mountain folks often carried in cages they'd set in the aisle for all to step over. As the combination started up a particularly steep grade, he considered jumping off and taking a walk through the rocks and trees along the tracks. Hell, he could probably climb the mountain afoot and be waiting up there, smoking another cigar, by the time his car screeched and groaned to meet him.

Then he remembered seeing the parlor car, usually stocked with hooch, fronting the highfalutin redhead's frilly pink demonstration of profound stupidity and decadence on wheels.

"What the hell am I doin' here?"

Longarm threw his cheroot stub out his open window, grabbed his rifle, and headed on out the coach's rear door. He took a deep drag of the cool air scented with the cinnamon of dead aspen leaves and pine resin, and strode through the next car back. He was glad not to have thrown down in this one, as there were a couple of dark-haired squawkers running up and down the aisle waving cottonwood sticks and imitating the sound of loud gunfire while their father snored under his floppy-brimmed hat and their mother, a pretty but dour-looking woman, had another one in a soiled white gown and bonnet suckling a droopy, red-mottled tit.

In the small but well-appointed parlor car, Longarm ordered a beer and a shot of Maryland rye from the middle-aged gent behind the makeshift bar that occupied the car's upper left corner, leaving the rest of the car free for a half dozen baize-covered card tables, a miniature roulette wheel, and even a dartboard. The windows were big, the sun was still bright though just now starting to wane, and the scenery was nice—columnar green pines and granite boulders—so Longarm sagged down in a padded chair behind a table near the car's largest window to enjoy the view with his boilermaker.

The saddle tramps he'd seen earlier, the car's only other customers, were drinking beers and playing a silent game of euchre on the other side of the jerking, lazily swaying car. They'd curse when the pitch of the grade would cause their beer schooners to slide down their table, but otherwise they sat hunched in the typically idle silence of the veteran cowpuncher.

Longarm had only just started to enjoy his hooch and view when the car's rear door opened to the rattle of the iron wheels hammering the track seams. He glanced back over his right shoulder, and his stomach soured. The four beefy, mustachioed gents dressed not unlike the bouncers in the Palo Duro Inn down in Texas sauntered in from the vestibule—one after another, one after another set of eyes sliding to Longarm in the car's shadows and holding.

The first gent was the oldest, with a broad, beat-up face, piercing blue eyes, and straw-yellow hair poking down from his brown bowler. He glanced over his shoulder at the three behind him and jerked his head to indicate Longarm.

"Aw hell," the federal lawman grumbled, sucking beer foam from his longhorn mustache and setting his schooner down on the table before him. "And here I was just startin' to have fun."

The four filed toward him, clenching their fists and rolling their shoulders like pugilists crawling through ropes into a ring.

Longarm forced a welcoming smile. "Howdy-ho, gents. Long time no see."

The redheaded bitch's four beefy bodyguards spread out around him, the oldest, blond hombre on Longarm's far left. The others were younger, but they all looked like they'd spent some time in a fight ring. The one whom the redhead had called Louis stood to the blond's right, and his hard gray eyes bore holes into the lawman who'd shown him such disrespect at Union Station.

They all wore sidearms that showed under their suit coats, but they seemed more inclined to use their fists, judging by how they were clenching them and polishing their knuckles as though they were the queen's rubies.

They glared down at their prey, who sat negligently back in his chair, one elbow hooked over his chairback, grinning dumbly up at them. He wanted no trouble. Of course, flashing his badge would likely waylay a dustup, but he hated to hide behind that nickel's worth of moon-and-star hammered tin. Avoiding trouble in such fashion was too costly to his pride.

The blond gent said in a faint Irish brogue, "Think you're a tough guy, do ya, now?"

"Oh, I reckon I'm tough enough. But back at the station I was just tryin' to keep from gettin' bowled over by you boys and that queen of fuckin' Sheba you're courtin'." To cover the insult that he hadn't been able to resist, he smiled and lifted his beer schooner once more to his mouth. "I didn't mean to get your necks in a hump, fellas. Say, why don't you belly up to the bar over yonder? First drink's on me."

"Think you're pretty goddamn funny, don't ya?" said the gray-eyed gent called Louis, hardening his jaws.

"Now, fellas," Longarm said with a chuckle, "that's the second question you've asked me, and to be honest, that one really ain't any easier to answer than the first. But if it'll keep your feathers combed, I'll give it a shot. I reckon I'm as funny as the next guy, when I'm in the mood for bein' funny. But when I'm not in the mood, I reckon you could probably get as big a laugh out of a crippled nun."

The blond gent and Louis shared a conspiratorial glance. Their chunky faces flushed, and their jaw hinges dimpled. The blond gent plopped down into the chair across from Longarm and leaned forward, resting his bulging, tattooed forearms on the table in front of him and letting his fingertips rest lightly on the scarred wood. He had a fat, jade pinky ring set in gold.

"You made me and my boys here look pretty foolish in front of our employer, now, didn't ya?"

"Questions, questions."

"Okay—here's one that might be a little easier to answer. Do you want us to smash your face to a bloody pulp, turnin' your nose sideways against your cheeks, or would you rather we break both your arms and your kneecaps? Fast now. We're not gonna give ya much time to ponder it. See, Miss Hathaway wants another bottle of wine, and me and the boys have fifteen minutes to throw down a couple o' beers and play some poker. So our time here is special, ya see, but we're willin' to spare a few extra minutes for you."

He grinned largely, showing snow-white teeth that were obviously false. "Answer quick now. It's one or the other."

Longarm sighed and turned his mouth corners down. "Jesus, fellas. Four against one just ain't fair!"

The blond gent spread his lips a little wider. "Who said anything about fair?"

"Well, if you're not gonna hold to fair, then me, the lone soldier here in this bailiwick, sure ain't neither!" With that, Longarm grabbed his beer schooner, swung it back behind his right shoulder, and rammed it forward against the blond gent's broad, scarred face with a loud thud of heavy glass against cheekbone.

The blond gent roared as the beer splashed over him and the glass slammed onto the table.

Spying a fist jutting toward him, Longarm leaned back in his chair and parried the blow with his right forearm, then bolted straight up out of the chair and rammed his head and shoulders into the gent who'd been standing on the far right end of the pack. The man, not expecting such quick movement from an hombre Longarm's size, stumbled backward, tripped over his own boots, and hit the floor on his back.

Getting his own boots beneath him and sensing the third and fourth men bounding toward him while the blond gent continued to bellow curses and hold his cheek over by the table, Longarm grabbed a chair and swung it around sideways with a furious grunt.

The chair slammed into the bodyguard with a checked suit and a lazy left eye. The man flew sideways, toward the back of the car, and Longarm found himself holding only the chair's broken back in his hands.

He looked at the gray-eyed gent he'd insulted in the Union Station. Louis stood before him, half crouching, boots splayed just over shoulder-width apart. He held his fists out in front of him, and he was grinning devilishly, one gray eye twitching with delight.

His grin brightened as, suddenly, he opened his right hand. There was a metallic click, and a long, slender, razor-edged blade jutted out from the man's hand, which he again clenched into a fist. The knife's fine, tempered steel winked in the light angling through the windows. Longarm could see the slender, black, spring-rigged sheath inside the man's right shirt cuff.

The gray-eyed gent shuffled toward Longarm, cocking his knife hand for a jab at Longarm's throat.

"Louis, no!"

Longarm thought for a moment the voice from Union Station was some kind of delayed echo inside his head. Then he saw Louis glance to his right, beetling his shaggy, black brows peevishly, and a little slackness settled in his shoulders as well as into the hand holding the knife slightly out from his body.

The woman's voice, pitched with anger, said, "What have I told you miserable louts about minding your manners? What you do when working for me is a reflection on me, and I won't be associated with gutter trash. Besides, I don't think you really want to knife a deputy United States marshal, now, do you, Louis?"

Longarm looked at the woman. She stood just inside the car's rear door, near where the lazy-eyed gent Longarm had hit with a chair was climbing to his feet and rubbing his shoulder, his shaggy, brown hair hanging in disarray around his paper collar. She returned Longarm's glance with a knowing one of her own, then regarded her paid apes once more as they stood, flushed and sullenly silent, expressions of incredulity etched on their savage faces.

"Yes, he's a federal lawman. I wouldn't blame him a bit if he threw all four of you damn privy rats in the federal penitentiary." She favored Longarm with another sharp glance, and Longarm found his loins responding to the high flush in her tapered, creamy cheeks, and the red sparks in her copper-brown eyes. "That would be the punishment, wouldn't it, Marshal Long? For assaulting a federal lawman?"

"I reckon if I wanted to see it that way." Longarm looked at the gray-eyed gent holding the knife halfheartedly. "But I reckon I'd prefer to see it as a personal matter. That way if this ugly mug doesn't put that knife back where it came from, I can feed it to him without having to worry about the paperwork."

The woman's voice grew harder as she tightened her jaws. "Put the blade away, Louis. And if I see it out again for any other reason than to parry an attack on me, you'll be heading back to the flea-bit Abilene brothel in which I found you hauling firewood and water for the sporting girls." She lifted her head to regard the blond gent holding a hand over the bloody gash on his right cheek. "You, Drake—do I make myself clear? If you and your men can't behave yourselves, you'll be dismissed."

Drake glanced at Longarm, his eyes still hard, enraged. Blood dribbled out from under his hand. Switching his gaze back to his high-blooded, no-nonsense employer, he nodded once.

"Get that cheek taken care of," the girl said. "No more scars, please, Drake. You look savage enough as it is. There's a fine line between looking tough and looking merely dumb and ugly. And I'll have that bottle of wine brought to my car at once." She glanced at the lazy-eyed gent clad in checked broadcloth. "Rafe, take care of it." She glanced at Longarm and arched a brow. "And a bottle of Marshal Long's preference. It's the least I can do to help square things here."

"Not necessary," Longarm said.

"Oh, but it is. Please, Marshal." Her brown eyes were beseeching, and her bosom heaved beneath her purple cape. "Do join me for a drink. It's the least I can do. Besides, I've grown quite bored with the conversation— if you can call it that—of these hired curs. All they've ever really learned to do is howl."

Chapter 6

Longarm hiked a shoulder, his loins tingling once more at the snooty bitch's regally tough charm accentuated by her incredible albeit haughty beauty. "I reckon it wouldn't be polite to turn you down, then, would it?"

She let the corners of her wide mouth rise as she turned to the bartender, who stood behind his liquor counter regarding the four bodyguards skeptically. "I'm sorry for the trouble, sir. I will pay for all damages. And do, please, enjoy a bottle of your preference on Miss Janice Hathaway."

"Thank you, Miss Hathaway," the barman said, nodding and flushing self-consciously. "That's right nice of you, ma'am. I hope I can sit in on one of your concerts one of these days."

"I'll see that you're given tickets good for whichever venue is most convenient for you, sir."

With that, she turned to Longarm. "Shall we, Marshal Long?"

Three of the four bodyguards slumped into chairs around a table near the bar, and the one whom the woman addressed as Rafe—the man whom Longarm had hammered with the chair—conferred with the bartender while the two saddle tramps stared at the vision in pearls and rubies in bashful silence. Longarm grabbed his hat and rifle from his table and turned to where the woman stood waiting for him in front of the parlor car's rear door.

Miss Janice Hathaway.

Damn. He should have known.

He'd read about the woman in the *Rocky Mountain News* and seen sketched likenesses of the singer whom the newshacks called the "Angel of the Rockies." Miss Hathaway traveled via rail, performing either solo or in small groups at the lavish little opera houses that had sprung up, improbably but lavishly, in many of the mining camps up and down the Rockies. But the sketches didn't even begin to do the girl's beauty justice. He'd heard she sang like a summer breeze through cottonwoods.

Shit, here she was in the flesh. And she'd invited him to her own personal railcar for a drink . . .

As though reading his mind, she smiled with satisfaction, opened and closed her eyes slowly, dipped her chin slightly, and said huskily, "Your preference, Marshal Long?"

Longarm stood frozen, staring at her fine neck, clean-lined jaws, and slightly upturned nose, his ear tips warming.

"That is, your drink preference, sir . . ." the girl added, her own blush reaching her temples.

"Oh." Longarm chuckled and turned to the bartender and Rafe. "Give me a bottle of Maryland rye."

With a touch of the insouciance that Longarm had witnessed in Union Station, Miss Hathaway swept her eyes across him once more—a quick but bold glance of appraisal—then swung around to the door and stopped, waiting.

Longarm hustled to open the door for her then ushered her out onto the vestibule, where the wind blew her hair delightfully and pressed her skirts against her long, slender legs and nicely formed ass. His heart thudding sharply, he slipped past her to open the door of her own private railcar, and once they were both inside, he closed the door, doffed his hat, and stood looking around in awe at the car's extravagance.

He'd never seen so much red velvet and brocade, and delicate little tables made out of obviously fine and probably rare wood and covered with lace doilies on which stood clocks, music boxes, ornately framed tintypes, and colored bottles and goblets. Two crystal chandeliers hung over the deep, plush carpet, at front and back. In the far wall, a dark, varnished door stood open to a bed that seemed to fill the entire small sleeping quarters and which was covered in a thick, wine-red comforter with thick pillows covers in the same material.

"Holy moly," Longarm cooed, looking around. "You sure do travel in style, Miss Hathaway."

"Oh, you mean this little thing?" The singer chuckled huskily, white teeth gleaming between ruby red lips. "Yes, I am rather spoiled, I guess. This is all compliments of the railroad, and I'm told the opera houses in Leadville and Central City chipped in. It seems that having the Angel of the Rockies arriving for her performances in her own private car is good for business." She indicated a red-and-gold-brocade feinting couch at the right side of the car, the car's largest piece of furniture, with carefully scrolled arms in the shapes of lounging lions. "Please, make yourself comfortable, Marshal Long."

A knock sounded on the door through which they'd just entered. Miss Hathaway turned to open it. She muttered something too softly for Longarm to hear above the loudening clatter of the iron wheels—they seemed to be on a slight forward downgrade—then closed the door and turned to Longarm with a bottle in each hand.

She held up the bottle of fancily labeled red wine and the Maryland rye as she strolled toward Longarm. "They're uncouth dullards with a nary an intelligent scrap of conversation amongst the four of them, but I can scare the hell out of them with a look, and they jump when I say frog!"

Longarm sat on the feinting couch while Miss Hathaway, from whose incredible hourglass figure Longarm could not detach his gaze, set the bottles on a round table on which sat a framed photograph of the actress herself in costume with some older gent also in costume and whose name Longarm should know but defied recollection. He didn't think about it long, as his eyes as well as the brunt of his thoughts were on the delicious-looking actress's round but not overly large bottom, the shape of which her thick, pleated skirts did little to hide.

She threw off her cape, jostling her earrings and the little sausage curls of lustrous red hair hanging along her jaws, and popped the cork on the Maryland rye.

"Just the whiskey, Marshal Long?"

"If you have a beer laying around too lonely for words—that'd be nice. Otherwise the whiskey will more than fulfill your debt, Miss Hathaway." Longarm frowned as he watched her fill a short green goblet with his favorite brew. "How do you know my name, anyway? If we'd run into each other before, I'd remember."

"Marshal Long, a lady must keep her secrets!" She laughed huskily as she turned, her skirts fluttering about her legs, and Longarm's breath caught in his throat when he saw that the front of her gown was so deeply cut that it revealed nearly all of the delightful if uppity creature's deep, creamy cleavage. Her breasts were large and in spite of the confining corset he could see that they were shaped like pears—large, lovely, branch-ripened pears growing in the most fertile of orchards.

With some effort, he raked his gaze from the actress's chest to the goblet she held before him in a fine-boned, manicured hand, noting absently in the yet-uncivilized part of his brain that high on her left orb was a faint, brown, heart-shaped freckle, which for a quarter second he imagined placing his mustached lips upon. "Much obliged."

"Actually," she said, turning away again with another intoxicating, fragrant swirl of her gowns and heading back to the table, "I inquired with the conductor."

Longarm sipped the rye that no doubt tasted like that which he'd sipped in the parlor car but which here in the girl's presence tasted like the prime nectar of the most gracious of gods. "Oh?"

"Of course." As she opened her wine bottle, she cast a bright, brashly flirtatious smile over her shoulder. "You must know that you're a rather striking figure, Marshal Long. Tall and darkly, ruggedly handsome. Right striking to the female eye."

"Ah, hell," Longarm growled, feeling his cheeks and ears warm again so that he felt like a love-struck boy kicking horse apples in the schoolyard dust. "You're gilding the old lily just a tad, but I reckon one would expect such from a famous actress."

"Not at all." She strode toward him with her half-filled crystal wineglass in her hand, a smoldering smile making her lustrous brown eyes sparkle and her ruby lips glow. "As a matter of fact, Marshal, I was trying for as much subtlety as I could muster . . . with such a handsome and, I might add, famous frontier law bringer as yourself sitting on my feinting couch."

"Famous? *Pshaw!*"

"As soon as I heard the name, I recognized it. Who hasn't heard of the famous Long Arm of the Law?" She folded as gracefully as a songbird onto the feinting couch, so close to Longarm that he could smell her and feel the wind of her fluttering skirts and dancing hair held in a loose French braid behind her head.

Taking her wineglass in her left hand, she propped her right elbow on the couch's back and crossed her legs, sort of squirming around and getting as close as she could without actually sitting on his lap. "I read about you in the *Policeman's Gazette*, Marshal Long. Quite a career you've had."

"Well, since you've read about me and I've read about you, why don't you go ahead and call me Longarm. I feel kinda funny being called Marshal all the time by a woman as beautiful as you, Miss Hathaway." He glanced at her cleavage once more, which seemed to be moving as though a snake were squirming around between those two perfectly formed orbs, then grinned up at her sheepishly.

She plucked a speck of wood ash from the lapel of

his black frock coat and bored his eyes with her own. "In that case, only Janice will do for me, Longarm."

"All right, then"—Longarm clinked his goblet against the actress's wineglass, too aroused to feel foolish about his blushing and carrying on like a Lutheran farmboy on his honeymoon—"Janice it is."

"And that?" she asked, sliding her smoky gaze to his crotch. "What do you call that?"

He followed her gaze to where his rock-hard shaft lay along his left thigh like a poorly concealed club in his pants. "That there, Miss Janice, is the hardest boner I've ever experienced, and I hope you won't be scandalized to learn I've experienced a few."

Miss Janice Hathaway lifted her glass to her lips, sipped her wine with a slight wet, sucking sound, and swallowed it hard. She brushed her free hand across his crotch and then plucked another piece of ash from his coat. "Would it help to take it out of there and give it some air? The poor thing's liable to suffocate—it being so big and those whipcord trousers being so snug."

"Why, Miss Janice. What would you think of me if I went whipping my cock out in the presence of a lady?"

She lifted her glass to mouth once more, pressed her lips to it, tipped it up, and swallowed. She continued to stare into his eyes as she reached down and set her glass on the floor beneath the feinting couch. She did the same with his glass and then sat down beside him again, closer this time, propping her right elbow on the couch back and placing her left hand, palm down, on the long, snake-shaped bulge on Longarm's thigh.

The sensation of her hand on him made his knees tingle. He groaned softly.

"If you're too shy to do it yourself, Longarm, would you like me to do it?" She snuggled still closer, brushed her nose against his jaw. "I hope you don't think me too forward, but I don't get many opportunities of this kind. The gentlemen you encountered earlier are really too stupid and ugly to have around for long, and they're too wrapped up in their silly old selves to perform well in a woman's boudoir. But when I saw you earlier, even before I knew who you were and remembered your reputation, I knew that you could do right well by a lady. I bet you could really throw the blocks to her and have her just about screaming like a fucking mare in the throws of foaling."

Longarm chuckled, genuinely shocked by the woman's frankness. "Miss Hathaway," he groaned as she pressed her hand down harder on his throbbing member, "such barn talk for a lady of your class . . ."

"Lady? Class? I'm an actress, Marshal." Her voice was a warm purr, and as she pushed her face to within an inch of his, he could smell the pleasant fragrance of red wine on her breath. She touched the tip of her tongue to his ear, and he gave a shiver of appreciation. "We're the very bottom of the societal food chain, don't you know? Hardly a step up from the sporting girls . . . which most of us were at one time. I, however, managed to escape that line of work and jumped right from my father's riverboat line, dancing and singing when I was only twelve, to the western opera houses. Somewhere along the way, however, I did manage to acquire an insatiable appetite for bedroom frolic . . . especially with big, rugged men . . . the kind of men who powered my father's stern-wheelers. I've never . . . uh, snuggled . . . with a lawman before—famous or well-hung or otherwise . . ."

As she'd spoken in her low, sensuous tones, she'd continued to flick her tender tongue into Longarm's ear and deftly unbuckled his cartridge belt as well as the buttons of his fly. Now he grunted as she slipped her hand inside his whipcord trousers, then through the fly of his balbriggans.

He grunted again, louder, when her cool hand touched his searing hard-on. His throat dried, and his tongue swelled. Her smile growing as she stared into his eyes, knowing full well the calamity she was causing inside him, she slid her hand slowly along the length of his cock to its head, then very gently slid it back toward his belly until it was standing at full mast from his crotch, angling slightly back toward his belly, throbbing.

"Now that," Miss Hathaway said, widening her eyes as her gaze slid to the throbbing, purple-headed member in her fine, pale hand, "is an organ!"

With that she dropped her head down to his crotch and lowered her mouth over his cock, her wildly flicking tongue and sliding lips feeling like warm, oozing mud. Longarm groaned, ground his heels into the deep plush carpet, and grabbed the edge of the couch with his fists, gritting his teeth as the woman's gorgeous head bobbed in front of him.

He soon found that Miss Hathaway was a true artist of the boudoir, for she managed to bring him to the very brink of climax and no farther before lifting her head, showing him her flushed cheeks, and raking the back of her hand across her wet, swollen lips.

"Now, that was fun," she wheezed, her chest rising and falling sharply. "But I believe it's time now to get down to some *serious* business!"

With that, she sat up and, staring at him hungrily, let him watch her reach behind to unfasten and untie the multitude of buttons, hooks, and strings that held the complicated puzzle of gown, shirtwaist, camisole, and corset together. Longarm's eyes bulged in amazement as the last garment fell away from her shoulders, exposing the breasts that were even more gorgeous and succulent than he'd imagined—fuller, riper, paler, with areolas as broad as his hand and tipped with jutting pink nipples.

He flung himself forward to bury his face in that warm, heaving bosom, and a few minutes later, he had her down on the floor, on her hands and knees, and, wearing only his hat, was taking her from behind like a raging stallion with his favorite mare in a shimmering field of summer clover.

That particular tumble lasted only a few short minutes, so heated were both parties. But the orgy was just beginning. In fact, Longarm never did return to his seat in the coach car, instead remaining virtually naked as the most decadent of Arab sheiks, in Miss Hathaway's private rolling digs as the combination snaked and climbed its way deep into the Rockies, through one little medieval-looking village after another, over one alpine pass after another, pausing only to exchange passengers before continuing between, through, and over the rugged, piny ridges.

Between bouts of lovemaking—if you could call the coupling of two wild, sex-crazy bobcats lovemaking—Miss Hathaway ordered her thugs, who were now confined to the parlor car where they likely drank and played poker and licked their physical and psychological wounds, to haul Longarm's gear to her rolling boudoir. In addition, over the course of the next three days and nights that passed for Longarm behind a fog of carnal intoxication, the actress had her dull-witted liege running for steaks, fruit plates, *carne seca*, ham sandwiches, cheese wheels, and several bottles of red wine, port wine, champagne, and, of course, ale and Maryland rye.

She and Longarm drank coffee in the mornings while feeding each other grapes and little squares of Swiss cheese.

Occasionally she'd attach a bit of cheese or a grape to one of her nipples or toes. Longarm would slowly nibble the grape or cheese square off the appendage of choice, working the actress into a squirming, mewling rage. When she was at the end of her tether, she took his by now piston-hard mast between her long dancer's legs and clamped her heels against his hips, pinning him down against her. Or she'd wrestle him onto his back and straddle him, sliding her dripping, red-furred snatch over the bulging head of his organ and start bouncing, slowly at first, up and down on her knees.

The rhythm of the bouncing would increase gradually while Longarm nuzzled the girl's flopping, swollen breasts and ground his heels into the mattress until, after maybe a half hour or forty-five minutes of the strenuous, blissfully agonizing tussle, they'd come together, the federal lawman shooting his seed deep into her expanding and contracting core while she bellowed throatily and threw her head back on her shoulders, digging her fingers so deeply into his upper arms that they often bled, though he never felt a thing anywhere but in his quavering, lightning-struck loins.

Late on the third afternoon of the slow but sweatily strenuous trek—for Longarm, at least—the naked federal lawman became vaguely aware of snow falling outside the windows of Miss Hathaway's private car. It grew to a near whiteout, and the wind hammered the sides of the train with blasts of high-mountain snow. He finished a meal and, smoking a nickel cheroot propped in Miss Hathway's bed, watched it fall more quickly and heavily.

He swept a curtain away from a window as he became aware of the crawling train jerking to a squawking stop. Outside, behind the veils of wind-thrashed snow, he could see the ghostly outlines of wooden buildings and stock pens situated amongst bending pines. They were entering a town, possibly his destination of Sully Creek. Because of the storm, it was hard to tell.

"Shit," he said, nibbling the cheroot as the snow pelted the window like sand, blocking his view. "Like I done warned Billy, I'm liable to get stuck up here till May!"

They'd just finished another romp, and the actress was lying belly down on the bed, near the crackling wood stove, naked as the day she was born and eating a tender, nearly raw steak.

"We both might, Custis," the actress said, swallowing. "Won't it be lovely?"

"Shhh."

"What is it?"

"You hear that?"

She frowned, her empty fork in front of her mouth. "I didn't hear any—"

It came again—a man's frantic yell.

It grew louder until a figure dashed in front of the window, materializing out of the storm.

Suddenly, a man's wide-eyed, horrified face shoved up so close to the frosty glass that Longarm could see the pores in the man's pitted skin and the individual hairs in his unkempt beard. He pounded the window with the heels of both hands, and Miss Hathaway screamed in horror, rising up from the bed and closing her arms over her breasts.

The man's voice was muffled behind the glass and beneath the moaning wind, but Longarm could hear him clearly. "Hep! Oh, Lordy, Marshal Long—hep uuussssssss! *The maniac's done struck again!*"

Chapter 7

Longarm dressed as fast as he could, which wasn't all that fast since he was starting from scratch, not wearing a single scrap of underwear, and since his duds were scattered throughout Miss Hathaway's private pink railcar. He found one boot tipped upside down over the snoot of the brass horse hanging above the door to her private bedroom, and his ballbriggans were in a tight little ball under the covers on her side of the bed, as she'd gotten a hankering to wear them once while they fucked.

When he'd finally pulled on and slipped into everything, and had stomped into his boots and buckled his shell belt and gun around his waist, he donned his fleece-lined mackinaw. Wrapping a scarf around his neck, he headed out into the blowing, drifting snow, the wind instantly sucking his air from his lungs and nearly ripping his hat from his head. Two men stood on the snowy brick siding before him—the train's engineer in a big buckskin mackinaw and with his billed watch cap tied to his head with a wool scarf, and the conductor, Avril

Hollis, whom Longarm knew from his many years of coming and going by way of the iron horse.

The snow was coming down in thick waves, so that he couldn't see much of the town before him and caught only brief glimpses of the steep, rocky, pine-studded canyon walls on either side of him. Beyond was the depot on his far left, which the Shay engine sat in front of, chugging loudly.

"Where's the crazy son of a bitch that stuck his head in my window?" Longarm yelled above the sighing, moaning wind.

Avril Hollis stepped forward. He wore a bulky blue coat and his traditional blue, leather-billed conductor's cap, and a heavy green scarf wrapped three times around his scrawny neck. Snow stuck to his round spectacles like spitballs. "Name's Rappaporte. He's the station agent. He's also the Sully Creek mayor. Said he was the one who sent for you. I told him you were back here."

The conductor tossed his head toward the pink railcar flanking Longarm, and even in the blowing snow Longarm could see a wry flush crawling up the man's weathered cheeks. "I warned him that you and the uppity songbird were probably doin' naughty, private things to each other, but he ran back here, anyway. He's in the depot now with a hot toddy. Poor son of a bitch was about to have a heart stroke."

"Over what?"

"Have a look."

Hollis jerked his head toward the depot, and he and Longarm started walking that way, with the engineer, a silent, blunt-faced, and ill-tempered man named Eugene Tibbs, following sourly along behind.

"I'm keeping everyone on the train for now," Hollis yelled to Longarm above the wind. "We can't go on because the rails are likely blocked in the canyon ahead. We barely made it this far. You probably wouldn't know, seein' as how you were so busy, but we had to stop twice to shovel the tracks ahead of us."

Hollis gave Longarm a reproving look, and Longarm gave a sheepish hike of his shoulder. "You might've pounded on the door if you needed help."

"And risk that catamount's wrath?"

"Her bark's worse than her bite."

"I reckon you'd know, Custis."

They moved up to the station house—a long, low building with a steeply pitched, shake-shingled roof—and Hollis opened the door, which the wind grabbed and threatened to annihilate. Longarm went in, stomping snow from his boots and swiping his hat against his thigh. It was cold and dark inside, no lamps lit. The big bullet-shaped stove in the middle of the waiting area hunched, black and silent. A single man occupied the place, sitting on one of the long benches at the far side of the room, flanked by two gray windows, a chalked timetable on the wall directly behind him. At least, it looked like a man sitting there, his head obscured by the shadows.

There was a clatter and shuffling of feet behind one of the two teller's cages at the far right end of the building, and presently the man who'd shoved his head up against Longarm's and Miss Hathaway's window clomped out a narrow door between the cages, swinging a lighted lantern.

"Jesus, Joseph, and Mary!" The man, whom Longarm took to be the stationmaster, Rappaporte, tipped a bottle back, then set it on the varnished oak counter behind him, swallowing loudly. Longarm couldn't see much more than the man's blanket-coated silhouette, but the stationmaster/mayor of Sully Creek appeared a short, wasted-looking hombre. He wasn't wearing a hat and his longish hair hung down the sides of his narrow skull.

He turned toward where Longarm stood with the conductor and the engineer. "You Marshal Long?"

"That's right. What's this all about, Mr. Rappaporte?"

"What do you mean—what's it all about?" Rappaporte swung his lantern in the direction of the gent sitting in the shadows against the far wall. "He's what it's all about. At least, what it's all about now. He's what damn near stopped my heart when I came on over from my harness shop to get ready for the train!"

He took another pull from the bottle and let the glowing lantern hang straight down by his side.

Longarm glanced at Hollis. Hollis glanced back at him, melting snow sliding down the conductor's round spectacles. Longarm drew a breath and strode forward. He took the lantern out of Rapporte's hand. With Hollis following him but the engineer remaining near the door, and Rappaporte remaining near the tellers' cages, Longarm tramped to the far side of the room and turned to walk between the benches, heading for the man in the shadows.

Uneasiness plucked at the short hairs along the back of the lawman's neck, Holding the lantern high when he was ten feet from the man in the shadows, Longarm realized why. He'd thought he'd been unable to see the man's head because of the deep shadows on that side of the room. But he'd been wrong.

The reason he hadn't been able to see the man's head was because the man's head had not been in its rightful place atop the man's shoulders. Instead, the head was resting in the man's lap, sort of cradled in the man's large, dirty hands.

Where his head had been until someone had unceremoniously hacked it off was a ragged clump of bloody skin. Blood had thickly matted the man's denim jacket and the patched denim trousers beneath the head's new, grisly resting place, between the man's two, large, grime-encrusted hands that rested atop his thighs, palms up.

The face on the head was set in a ghastly grimace, showing a full set of tobacco-stained teeth and glassy, brown eyes wide with horror. The hair on the head was long and dark, streaked with gray and hanging straight down between the dead man's spread thighs.

"Oh, hell!" Hollis turned away, covering his mouth with his wrist and stifling a retch.

Longarm chewed his mustache. "Who is he?"

Rappaporte said hoarsely. "Foyle Goody. Takes care of the place, splits wood an' such. Half-breed from up Wyoming way. Had a hole hereabouts but the color faded, so he's been doin' odd jobs for the past coupla years. Jesus Christ, look what that goddamn maniac did to him."

"What maniac are you talkin' about?"

"Why, the same one that killed old Matt Green and his deputy, Iver Hansen!"

Longarm stared down at the snarling face of Foyle Goody, who seemed to be staring at Longarm's right thigh as though he could see the face of his killer there. The tinny smell of fresh blood was thick in the cold air. To mask it, Longarm reached inside his coat to pluck a nickel cheroot from his shirt pocket, and stuck it between his lips, rolling it around with his tongue. He leaned forward to get a look at the back of Goody's head. "How do you know the same man who killed them killed this fella?"

"Well, good Christ, Marshal—I hope we don't have more than one killer skulking around town!"

"Hoping's one thing." Longarm raised his right hand to gently slide a lock of the dead man's hair away from his scalp, revealing a long, deep gash—the mark of a heavy, blunt object. Likely, he'd been knocked cold, maybe even killed, before his head had been hacked off. The decapitation hadn't happened here, as there'd be a lot more blood if it had.

Longarm turned to Rappaporte. "You know who saw him last?"

Rappaporte took another drink and lowered his bottle, sighing wetly. His eyes looked haunted. He extended the bottle to Hollis, who, his back facing Longarm and the dead man, grabbed it quickly and tipped it back.

Rappaporte said, "He lived alone out by the creek, but he might have been over to the saloon before he came here. I was in my shop."

"How were the other two killed?"

"Same damn way. The girl who found them'll never be the same."

"Heads cut off?"

"That's what I said, Marshal."

"Goody have any enemies you know about?"

"No more than anyone else."

"How 'bout the lawmen?"

"Hell, I don't know!"

"How many people in town right now?"

"A dozen or so, give or take."

"You know 'em all?"

"Pretty much. Don't know one who could do some-thing like that." Rappaporte's voice caught, and wincing, he shook his head quickly as if to rid the image of the dead man from his eyes.

"Any of 'em have a disagreement with Goody? A fight over a woman or cards? A mining claim?"

Again, Rappaporte shook his head. "None that I know about. Goody wasn't much of a talker, didn't mix much. Not even with the women. Everybody knew him, though. Hell, he's probably worked for everybody in town at one time or another—even the whores. Can't imagine he'd have chafed anybody bad enough to get his wick snuffed that bad. Shit, seems like the work of some damn ma-niac. Same one—"

"I know," Longarm said, cutting the man off as he strolled around the station, swinging the lantern pensively, "same one that killed the constable." He stopped and looked back at Rappaporte. "Where are they—the law-men?"

"Over to the undertakers. Ground's too damn froze to bury anybody till spring."

"What about the passengers, Custis?" This from Hollis, who stood near Rappaporte, looking nearly as bleached out and haunted as the station agent. The engineer, Tibbs, remained near the door in grim, vaguely impatient si-lence, equally nettled by the bad weather that was hold-ing up his train as by the killing that complicated his involuntary layover.

Longarm fired a match on his thumbnail and touched

the flame to his cheroot, puffing smoke. "Keep 'em on the train till I check things out." To Rappaporte, he said, "Best fetch the undertaker, have Goody hauled away. You know where he was killed?"

Rappaporte shook his head and, glancing owlishly once more at Goody, grabbed his bottle back from Hollis and took another pull. Ramming the cork back into his bottle, he moved to the station's town-side door. He paused for a moment, peering cautiously out the door's glass pane, then stepped out into the mewling storm, continuing to look fearfully around for the maniac.

When the door had whipped closed behind the stationmaster, Longarm looked at Hollis. "Make sure no one gets off the train until . . ."

The lawman let his voice trail off as the door facing the train opened, and two of Miss Hathaway's bodyguards entered—the blond gent, Drake, who now wore a nasty-looking scab on his right cheek, and the one with longish black hair and a lazy eye—Rafe. They wore heavy, expensive-looking wool coats, and their ears were red beneath the brims of their snow-covered bowler hats.

Rafe closed the door on the blowing snow, and Drake scowled at Longarm. Above his scarred cheek, his right eye was swollen. "Miss Hathaway wants to know what's goin' on."

Longarm took another puff from his cigar and said around it, "Tell her a man lost his hat, and she best stay on the train till we find who took it."

"Huh?" Rafe grunted.

Longarm returned his gaze to Hollis. "Make sure no one gets off the train until I say so, all right, Av?"

"You got it, Custis."

"Oh, and your telegraph in service?"

"Nope. Snow took it out a couple of hours ago."

"Damn," Longarm said, but he wasn't sure why. It would be nice to tell Billy he'd made it to Sully Creek safe and sound, but aside from sending his boss occasional progress reports, the wires were of little use. It wasn't like he could get help up here even if he needed it. Not in this weather.

As Hollis glanced once more at the dead man, he made his way around Miss Hathaway's thugs. Longarm headed in the opposite direction, lifting his coat hem above the handle of his .44-40 as he tramped out into the wind through the door on the station's other side. He stood on the platform under the depot's overhanging roof, staring straight east along the canyon.

The hair under his collar pricked with an unnamed dread.

Chapter 8

Rows of private dwellings and business establishments stood on each side of the canyon, at the bases of the high, cloud- and snow-obscured ridges. The structures faced one another across Sully Creek's main drag that followed the canyon bottom as it meandered east, away from Longarm standing on the depot building's stoop.

As the lawman remembered from his one and only visit, about a mile beyond the town's far edge, the canyon doglegged back to the right and got even narrower, the walls even higher. That's where an older section of the village lay, moldering in old mine tailings and boulders tumbled from the ridges.

The snow danced in gauzy curtains, intermittently blocking out the frame shacks and shanties and the high, narrow, false-fronted business establishments. Shingle chains screeched beneath the wind's eerie mewling, and Longarm could hear the buildings creak and see for a few seconds a couple of dislodged shake shingles blow past. Faintly, he could pick up the occasional patter of a piano, but he couldn't tell exactly where it was coming from.

He sucked at his cigar, inhaled nothing but cold air. The wind had put it out. He kicked at the downy snow that had blown in beneath the depot's overhanging roof. A good ten inches so far, and it was still coming down.

Again, unease pricked at him.

Likely, despite Rappaporte's worries, the killer had had beefs with the lawmen and Goody, the half-breed. But the prospect that the stationmaster was right, and that there was a random killer on the loose in the canyon, where the train was stalled and the passengers were trapped with the dozen or so villagers, one of them being a kill-crazy maniac, caused Longarm's belly to dip dreadfully.

He turned to the left and walked along the station building, looking around for the killer's sign. He came to the end of the building, swung left again, and stopped, staring at the large pile of split wood—pine mixed with hardwood and cottonwood—stacked neatly against the station's log wall. There was a chopping block capped with snow, and a long-handled maul poking up out of it, also limned with snow.

In a large, irregular area round the base of the chopping block, the snow was slushy, as though warmed from below.

Longarm hitched his trousers up his thighs and dropped to a knee. He removed his right glove and shoved a finger into the wet snow, raised the finger for inspection. The melting snow was oily and red. Blood. Goody had been killed out here, likely when he'd come out to gather wood for a fire, intending to have the depot warm for the soon-to-be-arriving passengers.

Longarm looked around at the large, slushy blood pool, then picked up a length of split cottonwood. A sharp edge of the pale wood was blood-smeared, and a few strands of gray-brown hair clung to the blood. He tossed away the chunk of wood the killer had obviously used as a club and looked around, continuing to roll his cold cigar from one side of his mouth to the other.

About fifty yards beyond the depot building's corner stood a big, boarded-up barn, obviously abandoned. There was a corral out back, grown up with tall, dead grass and tumbleweeds that the snow was quickly covering. Between the station and the barn were a large boulder and a wind-gnarled cedar tree. Whoever had killed the half-breed may have been hiding behind the barn, waiting for him to come and ready the station for the train, then stole up behind the man, using the boulder and the fir tree for cover before creeping in close and blowing Goody's wick with the cottonwood log.

Judging by how much snow had melted into the blood, the killing had probably happened less than an hour ago.

Whatever the killer had used to hack off the man's head he'd apparently taken it with him, for no such instrument remained near the woodpile.

"Where are you, you son of a bitch? And why'd you cut the poor bastard's head off? Just your sense of humor? Wanting to give the train passengers a shock, were ya?"

Longarm switched his thoughts from the killer's motives to finding the man himself, because the only answer to his questions could be that the man was, as the stationmaster feared, a raving lunatic. No, he wouldn't get inside the man's head. He'd just take a tramp up the street and see what he could see. All tracks were likely obliterated, but he might find something the killer had left behind.

Or, hell, he might even run into the killer himself. Sometimes the real crazy ones liked to hang around and enjoy the befuddlement they caused in those trying to track them. That didn't mean that Longarm had a maniac on his hands, though. He wouldn't give up hope that the killer had had very particular reasons for killing the lawmen and Goody, and that now that he'd aired his spleen and had his laugh, he'd turn his horns in.

Hitching his shell belt up higher on his hips, Longarm headed out away from the depot building, tramping on past the barn and scuffing through the snow along Sully Creek's main drag, staying to the left of the narrow stream that ran down its middle and which was still open, its swirling water blackly cold with a few snow chunks bobbing to and fro around the rocks and down the tiny falls.

He paused to pin his badge on his coat. He usually wore the badge only when making an arrest, but it couldn't hurt to have folks knowing a lawman was around. Of course, it might scare the killer into making a brash move, but if that move was made on Longarm, all the better.

He continued up the canyon, the floor of which sloped upward slightly, the gurgling stream on his right, private cabins, and false-fronted business establishments on his left—all constructed of heavy, hand-axed logs. Keeping his hat tipped low against the wind, his left arm snugged against the .44-40 holstered on his left hip, he approached a cabin with elk antlers nailed above the door.

Between the antlers and the door frame was a wood shingle into which MISS TULIP had been burned.

As Longarm continued straight up the canyon, the cabin door opened with a wooden scrape, and a young, blond woman poked her head out as she held a shaggy buffalo robe tight about her shoulders. She had a fleshy, gray-eyed face that fell somewhere between plain and attractive, but her smile was toothily seductive, and it caused her smooth, pale cheeks to dimple. "Come in out of the cold, sweetheart!"

Longarm stopped and pinched his hat brim to her. Her eyes flicked across his badge, and her sandy brows beetled with a vague disappointment as she slid her gaze back toward the depot station behind him. "You ain't the only one that got off here, are ya, lawdog?"

"So far." So he wouldn't have to yell above the wind, Longarm tramped through the snow and stopped a few feet away from the girl poking her puzzled head out the door. "Miss, have you seen anyone else moving up canyon from the depot within the last hour or so?"

She returned her gaze to Longarm, her frown deepening, her eyes turning skeptical. "Why you askin'?"

"'Cause a man named Goody got himself beefed down there about an hour ago, and I'm looking for his killer."

"Ah, shit! Goody's dead?"

"Yes, ma'am."

"Ah, shit, shit, shit!" The girl cursed loudly, bobbing her head for emphasis and hardening her jaws angrily. "He brought wood in for me this mornin', just after sunup!" She glanced back at the depot again. "Shit! Shit! Shit!"

Longarm looked down at the girl. He could feel the

warmth of a hot fire emanating from the cabin behind her. He picked up the aroma of fresh tea, baking buns, and salt pork. "You seen anyone head past here?"

"No, I ain't seen no one. Not in the last coupla hours, anyway."

"You know of anyone who had an ax to grind with Mr. Goody?"

She seemed offended by the question. "Hell, no! He hardly spoke two words to anyone, much less cursed anyone out. He didn't drink or play cards. Just worked. Damn hard. Shit, now who'm I gonna get to chop my wood for me?"

"Ma'am, you said—"

"Call me Tulip," the girl interrupted him, her expression softening as she stared up at the tall, buckskin-clad lawman before her. "Everyone around here does. You wanna come in for a minute, git yourself warm? My winter rates are the best in the canyon."

"I bet they are. No offense intended."

"You got a name, Marshal?"

"Call me Longarm. I'd love to stay and chat, but I'm gonna look around, see if I can find the son of a bitch who killed your woodcutter, Miss Tulip."

"You do that," she said, angry again. "Shoot the son of a bitch."

Longarm started to turn away but then, thinking of something, turned back to the frisky sporting girl. "Say, Miss Tulip, you said you haven't seen anyone come by here in the last coupla hours. How 'bout before that? Anyone who looked suspicious—maybe someone who looked angry or nasty or had blood on 'em."

"Nope, no one like that, Longarm. The only man I

seen out today, it bein' a stormy Sunday an' all, was Miss Wilomena's customer." The girl jerked her head up and back, indicating a gray cabin perched on a slope behind Miss Tulip's humble digs. "He's been there since early this mornin'. Ain't seen no one out and about since, except for poor Foyle Goody, I mean. Damn the son of a bitch that killed him!"

"Do you know the gent with Miss Wilomena, Miss Tulip?"

"Of course. Parson Fitzgerald."

When Longarm narrowed a skeptical eye, the girl chuckled. "Sure as shit—the parson's Miss Wilomena's most regular winter customer. Likes to take advantage of her winter rates, I reckon. His old feet probl'y need warmin', and she keeps a hot fire. The parson'll wander on over to the Trinity soon, spend the rest of the day huddled there by the fire. That's where you'll find most everyone else in town, Longarm. 'Ceptin' a hermit or two. I'd say if Goody's killer is still around, and I don't see how he could get out of town in this weather"—she looked around and shivered inside her buffalo robe— "unless he had wings and blew on down to Mexico, I'd say he'll be holed up over there, drinkin' himself warm with everyone else."

"I believe I remember the Trinity." Longarm pinched his hat brim to the girl. "Obliged, Miss Tulip. Go on in and get warm."

"Come on back anytime, Longarm. I got me a hot fire, too—both inside and outside, if'n you get my drift!"

Longarm laughed as he tramped up the street, bent into the wind. "I do at that, Miss Tulip, and I might just be takin' you up on them winter rates soon!" He threw

an arm up in farewell and concentrated on keeping his
low-heeled cavalry boots from slipping out from under
him in the slick snow covering a sudden upgrade in the
canyon floor.

He passed several more shacks and two- and three-
story business buildings creaking in the wind that seemed
to be howling louder as it blew down the canyon. He
spied the stationmaster, Rappaporte, push out between
the two, big double doors of a low wagon shed under the
sign for ENGEL'S FINE FURNITURE AND UNDERTAKING.
The stationmaster held his coat closed with both his
gloved hands and, kicking through the heavy snow and
appearing too miserable to even lift his head toward Longarm on the other side of the creek, began trudging back
in the direction of the train station and the stalled narrow-
gauge combination.

He disappeared quickly in the snow whipping down
at a slant.

Longarm crossed a snowy wooden bridge, one of
several that stretched across the rocky, meandering creek
along the main drag, and stood before a sprawling log
building with a wide front stoop and a second-story balcony. Large green letters painted across the false facade
announced BILL CARSON'S TRINITY SALOON AND HOTEL.

It was a big, solid-looking structure, with several wind-
jostled rocking chairs on the porch, and it appeared nearly
black against the falling snow and the cloud-obscured
ridge wall rising behind it. The piano music he'd heard
earlier had doubtless come from here, but the piano
had fallen silent. It was been replaced by loud thuds and
wild laughter.

Longarm tramped up the front steps, noting the lack

of tracks in the several inches of fresh snow, and crossed the stoop to push through the heavy storm door, a cowbell clattering loudly above his head. As warm air rich with the smell of wet wool, leather, liquor, and cured meats pushed against him, he saw a half dozen men surrounding the large, iron-banded potbellied stove in the middle of the cavelike room, with one more sitting right of the small group, laying out a card game on the table before him.

Two more were jostling around in the room's rear shadows, but Longarm's eyes were slow to adjust from the white snow glare, and he couldn't see what they were doing back there exactly, only hear the din of laughter and the stomping of fast-moving boots along with what sounded like a wheezing imitation of a horse's neigh.

Chapter 9

All heads turned toward Longarm as he closed the door behind him, staring straight ahead. The cowbell clattered silent.

Beyond the group sitting on chairs around the stove, he saw two others moving into a vague gray patch of window light on the scuffed wooden floor. Longarm thought the light and shadows was playing a trick on him—but no, the tall, broad-shouldered gent with a hawkish nose and long black hair and a long black beard really was carrying a scrawny, silver-haired gent up high on his shoulders, and the scrawny gent was flapping his elbows as his hands clutched the tall man's coat collar and his boots ground into the tall gent's ribs.

The two men were laughing hysterically beneath the thunder of the tall man's hammering boots.

They were swinging toward the front of the room, the tall man lifting another raucous whinny and the scrawny gent said, "Take me home now, you miserable cayuse!" when the tall gent's laughing eyes found the stranger stand-

ing at the front of the room, likely silhouetted against the
window in the door behind him.

The tall man imitating the horse stopped, staring,
the smile slowly dying on his lips. At the same time, the
scrawny gent also swung his gaze toward Longarm, and
the two stood or sat frozen for a moment, scrutinizing
the badge-wearing stranger before the scrawny gent said,
"You get here on the train, there, lawdog?"

"It'd be a long walk from Denver."

"You the federal Rappaporte wired?"

"One and the same."

Still perched on the shoulders of the tall bearded man,
and not seeming a bit self-conscious about it, the scrawny
gent, who had a red, bulbous nose and close-set eyes set
beneath a high, clean forehead, said, "You the only one
that got off?"

Longarm was raking his gaze across the men gathered around the stove, wondering if the killer was amongst
them. "So far."

"What the hell do you mean, so far?" The scrawny
gent smacked the top of the tall, bearded gent's head
with the back of his hand. "Down, Sylvus!"

The "horse" leaned forward to deposit the small man
gently on the floor, flat-footed.

Longarm slid his gaze across the scrawny gent staring up at him, who couldn't have been much over five
foot three even in his high-heeled stockmen's boots, to
the lone cardplayer laying out a game of solitaire.

The loner wore a heavy buffalo coat. His long, tangled, sandy hair hung straight down his shoulders, obscured his down-canted face. When the man looked up
at Longarm, the lack of facial hair and something about

the directness of the person's eyes caused Longarm to doubt that he was a man at all, but possibly a woman—a rather unattractive, middle-aged woman with rawboned, rugged features and a silver eyetooth that glistened in the light from a near window. The hands on the card deck were large but finer-boned that a man's, though the fingernails were every bit as grime-crusted.

A loosely rolled quirley smoldered in an ashtray just right of her neatly arranged cards.

Longarm looked back at the scrawny gent scowling up at him. "The passengers'll stay on the train for a bit. The stationmaster found a man murdered in the depot. Foyle Goody."

Longarm paused as he catalogued the reactions of the men sitting around the stove and those of the scrawny gent and the tall bearded gent, Sylvus, who'd slumped down at a table to splash whiskey into a beer schooner. The tall man was now tipping the schooner back, drinking thirstily while rolling a curious eye around the glass at Longarm.

The loner stared at Longarm, too, and when he or she had seemed to absorb the information, she blinked her eyes slowly and gave her a head a shake before returning her attention to her game.

"Fuck," said the scrawny gent. "Goody's dead?"

"Had his head cut off and set in his lap like a pumpkin in a garden patch." Longarm stepped forward, continuing to look around at the men facing him, and at the mannish-looking woman playing solitaire. He got no sense of either guilt or innocence from anyone—mainly just incredulity and an understandable guardedness in the presence of an outsider, and a lawman outsider at that.

The only one he got a decidedly odd sense from was a big, bald gent sitting left of the stove and with a black cat with a curled tail on his broad right shoulder. He was a stocky, strong-looking hombre, clean-shaven but with small, belligerent eyes that had been riveted to Longarm since Longarm had first entered the saloon. Hands like pale roasts rested on his thighs. He was big enough, and he looked mean and wicked enough, to do what had been done to Foyle Goody over at the train station.

Far back in his eyes, as though behind a second, inner lid, he seemed to be smiling.

"You fellas all been here for a while?" Longarm asked.

"Shit, I been here since last night," said the person of indeterminate sex in a high, raspy voice that further convinced Longarm she was a she. Ugly females populated these towns the same way mean-looking, hammer-headed male cusses like the bald gent did—in droves.

Longarm floated his glance across the hard, liquory-eyed, bearded faces around the stove, and let it snag on the bald gent, who was still staring at him like he was a side of beef that the ham-fisted gent was yearning to chop into roasts. "How 'bout the rest of you?"

"No one here killed Goody, Marshal," the scrawny gent said. "I know these boys . . . and Flora there." He glanced at the long-haired solitaire player who continued placing cards on the table with soft snicking sounds. "We all been here since early this mornin'. There ain't much to do in Sully Creek even when the weather's good, 'cept drinkin' and fuckin', so the boys and Flora drink here most of the day then head on over to the whores' cribs to fuck away the night."

"Except for Flora here." Flora sucked a deep drag from her quirley. Blowing smoke at the rafters, she said, "When I need a fuck I just go on upstairs with Bill, bang his brains for him good."

The others laughed or chuckled sheepishly, as though at a bawdy joke told in church. Bill flushed and looked a little appalled. Flora laughed loudly, hoarsely at her own joke, showing that silver eyetooth again, and let her ironic gaze settle on Longarm. "But now that you're here, lawdog, I might just give Bill a little rest."

"Shut up, Flora," Bill scolded the woman. To Longarm, he said, "Whoever killed Goody likely killed the constable and his deputy, Iver Hansen. If he ain't in here—and he ain't, I tell ya, and I run this here saloon so I'd know—he's likely still out there somewhere. And I for one don't like the idea of bein' shut up in this canyon durin' a storm—one that looks to last a couple days at least—with a howlin' fuckin' maniac runnin' off his leash."

"Settle down, Bill," Flora said as she perused her cards, cigarette dangling from her mouth. "I'll protect you."

A couple of the others chuckled. Longarm kept his eyes on the big, bald gent, who held Longarm's gaze with his own.

"How 'bout you, friend?" Longarm didn't care who he offended. He had a trainload of stranded passengers to worry about, and this man could have easily blown Goody's wick with a single swipe of that cottonwood log. "You been here all mornin'?"

The bald gent smiled, his big, clean, golden-brown face and his egg-shaped head crinkling with deep lines. "Sure, I have." He had a burly voice to go with his burly physique, and he was missing several teeth. "You think you can prove otherwise, you prove it."

The cat on the big man's shoulder leaped to the floor with a thud and disappeared into the saloon hall's chill, dank shadows, mewling.

"Shut up, Scotty," Bill admonished. "Can't you see the man's tryin' to do his job? In case you ain't thought about it, whoever killed big Foyle Goody has gotta be one mountain of a mean son of a bitch, and we're in a helluva lot of trouble if the bastard's still on the prowl."

Bill had shuffled up to the big front window right of the door, flanking Longarm, and he was looking in both directions along the street, nervously running his thick, brown hands along his bandy, denim-clad legs. "Well, looks like the killer spared the parson, anyways."

As if to punctuate his sentence, there was a boot thump on the porch steps. Longarm turned as the door opened, and a tall, gaunt gent with a salt-and-pepper mustache and untrimmed goatee shambled in, wearing buckled rubber boots over his shoes, and a long, black horsehair coat and tophat. A bottle jutted from one pocket of his coat. As he removed his hat and closed the door, he turned to Longarm and let his lower jaw hang, obviously surprised by the face of a stranger here in Sully Creek. Recovering, he smiled broadly, his hollow cheeks caving in even more, and said in a rumbling, resonant tenor, "Greetings, friend, and welcome to our fair city. I'm sure you're aware that the Lord Jesus Christ died for your sins, but if you're ever in doubt and fumbling in utter darkness, aware of neither where you've been or where you're going, or wondering why in the devil you were ever placed here in the first place, just tap on my door."

He pointed a long crooked finger at the ceiling. "Room two at the top of the stairs. Don't forget to bring a bottle!"

"I'll remember that, Parson."

"And speaking of bottles," the parson said, turning to the scrawny saloon man still staring out the window. "Bill, this poor soldier has gone to his reward. Would you be so kind as to provide reinforcements?"

Looking nettled, Bill grabbed the empty bottle that the parson proffered and strode bull-legged off to the long mahogany bar at the rear of the room and over which three trophy heads—two mountain rams and a snarling grizzly—loomed.

"How was Miss Wilomena, Parson?" asked one of the men sitting around the fire—a stubby, red-haired man in a red-and-black-checked shirt who was playing an idle game of checkers with the man beside him.

"Round and supple." The parson tossed his hat on an antler tree by the door, then walked over and turned his butt to the stove. "By God, gents, when I lay with that woman—stroke those full, round breasts and run my hands down those spectacular haunches—I become a believer all over again!"

The men laughed.

Flora howled, blowing smoke at the ceiling.

Meanwhile, Longarm strode over to the window left of the front doo, and, only vaguely hearing the buoyant, drunken conversation behind him, stared into the snow-swept street, at times barely able to see the false-fronted buildings and shacks on the other side of the creek.

He'd considered rousting a couple of the saloon patrons to help him scour the town for the killer, as he'd become convinced the man was not amongst the crowd here. The man called Scotty had the size for the grisly job but not the temperament. The bald brute was hard and tough, and he could probably kill in a fit of rage, but he would not instigate the trouble nor have reason to murder a man who, by all accounts, was a guileless servant to the entire village.

Scotty killed men like Scotty himself, not men like Foyle Goody. Nor men like the two local lawdogs, unless, of course, he was raging drunk, but then others would probably have known about it.

Longarm was so deep in thought that he'd only vaguely heard the scuffing footsteps behind him. Someone touched his shoulder. He turned to see the scrawny, gray-haired man standing beside him, extending a filled shot glass.

"Here ya go, Marshal. Do you good. I'm Bill Carson, owner of these digs, and I reckon I ain't got around to welcoming you here to Sully Creek." He smoothed his center-parted hair down with his gnarled, red hands. "It ain't good news that Goody's dead. Not good news at all. I figured our trouble might just go as far as Green and Hansen—like maybe some drunk drifter killed 'em cause they wanted to lock him up or somethin', but ... shit, this looks bad." He looked out the window. "And with the weather bein' bad, too, it looks even worse."

"It don't look good," Longarm admitted. "This the only hotel in town?"

Carson nodded. "I got eight rooms. Anyone who doesn't mind the parson's snoring is welcome."

Longarm threw back his entire shot of the rotgut panther piss and said in a pinched voice, "How much per head?"

Carson looked away, running a couple of fingers across his lips with a sheepish air. "Three dollars is . . ."

"Too much."

Carson scowled at Longarm. "Well, shit, it ain't exactly like there's anywhere else them folks can stay!"

"Yeah, you got a monopoly, Carson. You sure as hell do." Longarm arched a schoolmasterly brow at the cunning saloon/hotel owner. "And if you take advantage of it by exploiting the stranded train passengers, I'll have to use my authority to confiscate the premises. You see, the train's haulin' the U.S. mail, and we're gonna need a secure place to store it until the storm passes."

The diminutive Carson shoved his long nose up at the lawman towering over him, balling his red fists. "You can't do that!"

In fact, Longarm wasn't sure he could do it. But whether he could or not, he would do it if he had to.

He said, "Fifty cents seems about right, seein' as how you're likely to make a killing off your hooch. But if you push it, I might even have to confiscate that, seein' as how the mail will be here an' all, and it wouldn't be prudent, having men drinkin' around the holier-than-thou U.S. mail. They might get drunk and snoopy and want to read Aunt Emma's letters to Cousin Ike and whatnot."

Carson's cheeks and eyes swelled as though a balloon were being blown up inside his skull. He hardened his jaws and gritted his teeth, grunting and sighing, his broad chest rising and falling like a blacksmith's bellows.

Longarm just stared down at the man, his face placid but his eyes severe, and finally, the saloon owner released the air in his lungs with a loud *whuff!* and, grabbing Longarm's empty shot glass out of the lawman's hand, wheeled and stomped in his bandy-legged gait back past the men and one lady gathered near the stove to the bar.

Longarm pinched his hat brim to Miss Flora, who was grinning at him from her table, and headed out into the storm. He hoped like hell the maniac wouldn't strike again until he got the passengers safely secured in their rooms.

Chapter 10

Longarm hoofed it through the snow on the south side of the main street, noting that it seemed to be coming down even harder than before, the gusts so strong they nearly blew him over and left him breathless.

Even the buildings closest to him, on his left, frequently disappeared behind the buffeting white curtains. Some structures creaked as though nails were popping from their seams. Shingle chains whipped raucously, and somewhere in the north, a loose door was banging free against its frame.

The only person Longarm saw on the street was a man driving a buckboard wagon and having to whip his reins savagely over the back of the single, frightened horse in the traces. As the wagon passed, moving up from the depot, the man bellowing angrily behind the scarf wrapped tightly around his face, Longarm saw a humped shape beneath a bobcat hide in the box.

Longarm found Rappaporte standing outside the depot's front door, under the groaning overhang. The man had a big pistol shoved down in his coat pocket, the walnut grips jutting visibly.

Longarm yelled above the moaning, groaning wind, "Everything all right over here?"

"Fine as the hair on a snake's ass."

"I see the undertaker hauled Goody away. Anyone see him, know about the killing or your so-called maniac?"

"I didn't tell nobody. Don't think Hollis would. Doubt Tibbs did, either, since Tibbs don't say nothin' to nobody."

"Let's keep it that way. Don't want a damn stampede."

Longarm followed the stationmaster into the station that was warm now from the fire in the potbellied stove and also rife with the smell of fresh blood. Hollis sat on one of the benches, leaning forward with his elbows on his knees.

As Longarm slapped snow from his hat and stomped it from his boots, he turned to Rappaporte, "You got a good long length of rope?"

The stationmaster was in a sour mood. "What the hell you want rope for?"

"I want the passengers to all get a good grip on it as they walk together up to Carson's place. Any old or young ones might get blowed down an alley."

"Good idea, Custis," Hollis said, pushing himself heavily to his feet and buttoning his coat. "Looks like it's getting worse out there. Any sign of the killer?"

"Nope. He's likely still in the village, though. The saloon looks all right. Let's get the passengers headed that way, but keep mum about the killing. Don't want anyone goin' loco and start shootin' at imaginary maniacs."

While Rappaporte went grumbling off in search of rope, Longarm followed Hollis out the depot's trackside door. Hollis climbed onto one of the passenger cars, and Longarm tramped back to the frilly pink car housing Miss Hathaway behind a gauzy blur of slanting snow. As he climbed the vestibule steps, he saw that his tracks of only forty-five minutes ago were filled in with fresh snow.

Longarm gave the car's door a single knock before going in. Two of the thuggish bodyguards—Drake and Rafe—standing in front of the door, pointed cocked pistols at him. Longarm raised his hands and grinned at the testy men, and they slowly, reluctantly let the revolvers sag while their expressions remained confrontational.

Miss Hathaway pushed between them to regard Longarm with a stern look of impatience. "Custis, what in the hell is going on here? My men said someone's been killed, and the tracks are blocked. Does that mean we're stranded here . . . with a killer running free?"

"That's pretty much the high and low of it, Janice. But I'd appreciate your not letting the cat out of the bag. The less the other passengers know of the situation, the better." Longarm pushed past the bodyguards gathered around the door, a couple smoking, one holding a drink in his hand, as he fetched his rifle and saddlebags.

"Well, what's happening?" Janice wanted to know.

To the bodyguards, Longarm said, "You fellas escort the lady up the street to the Trinity Saloon and Hotel. Nearly all the way through town, on the right side of the creek. You can't miss it between wind gusts. The stationmaster's fetching a rope for them that need it, so hold on, Janice. It's right nasty out there."

Slinging his saddlebags over his shoulder, he headed for the door.

Janice stomped her foot behind him, and he glanced back to see her staring at him, copper eyes blazing, cheeks flushed with exasperation. "Custis, you will kindly address me and not them! I will not leave my car. I'll wait out the storm right here."

"Best not do that. I can keep an eye on you over at the hotel. Out here, in this little ole car . . ."

"I'll be quite safe." Janice glanced at her thugs.

"Suit yourself."

Longarm turned once more to the door, pushing past the bodyguards who regarded him snidely, smugly. He opened the door and glanced once more at the actress, who stood behind her bodyguards, flushed and uncertain. "If you change your mind, you know where to find the rest of us. Don't wait too long, though. Gonna be dark soon."

He went back out onto the vestibule. The other passengers, hunched against the cold and all bulkily clad for warmth, were rushing across the platform and into the warmth of the depot building. Hollis was holding the door. The crowd seemed fairly thin—maybe a dozen passengers at most. Winter didn't see much train travel in these parts.

Longarm looked around carefully, making sure the maniac or whoever in hell the killer was wasn't skulking around the train, waiting to drag off one of the passengers. He clung to the hope that the killer had had personal beefs with the lawmen and Goody and wasn't some moon-touched savage eager to kill anything on two legs—but he'd best be ready for anything.

Seeing no one on the train's left side, Longarm stepped off the private car's vestibule and glanced back at the car's windows that showed light behind their cream, gold-tasseled shades and shadows moving around. He was reluctant to leave Janice here, but she was probably as safe here with her four thugs as she'd be in the hotel.

Longarm started toward the depot and stopped. Only one man remained on the platform—the burly engineer, Tibbs, shaped like a fawn-colored snowman in his soiled and scorched buckskin mackinaw, a black skullcap show-ing along the edges of his billed watch cap tied to his head with a scarf. He stood stiffly up near the wood ten-der, arms hanging at his sides, mittened hands resem-bling black clubs.

Longarm beckoned to the man, who shook his head. "Gonna stay here with the train," he bellowed just loudly enough for Longarm to hear above the wind.

"Come on over to the hotel, Tibbs," Longarm called. "It ain't safe out here."

"I'll stay in the station."

"You'll be alone. Rappaporte's likely heading home as soon as the passengers are squared away." Longarm beckoned again. "Come on, goddamnit!"

"All right," Tibbs said. "What about the mail?"

"It'll be safe here," Longarm assured him, in spite of his threat to Bill Carson.

Tibbs shrugged. "I'll get my gear."

As Tibbs turned toward the engine that sat silent and all but invisible behind the wildly falling snow, Longarm tramped on into the station.

"Anyone ask about the blood?" he asked Rappaporte, who stood looking out the window over the door.

"Nah, they were too cold."

"Good."

The stationmaster turned away from the window. He held a smoking stone mug in his gloved hand. The stove ticked softly; it was colder in the station than it had been a few minutes ago. Obviously, Rappaporte was letting the fire die. "You don't think they should know? I'd wanna know . . . if I didn't know already."

He frowned and stared owlishly into his coffee mug that had probably been laced from the corked bottle standing on the lip of one of the teller cages. "Nah, maybe not. Wouldn't sleep for shit . . . just like I ain't gonna do if I go home."

He turned to look out the window once more, at the shaggy string of passengers making their way up the street toward the hotel. Only two women, one child, and a stoop-shouldered old man were holding the rope as they blurred quickly into the whiteness. Beneath the howling wind, Longarm could vaguely hear one of the women speaking in a sharply admonishing tone to the child, who apparently didn't want to hold the rope—probably a boy who thought it was sissy.

"Think I'll go over and see Miss Tulip," Rappaporte said with a sigh. "She'll take my mind off this dark turn of events. In the spring, I might just light the hell out of here. I'm getting damn tired of the mountains, anyway. You know, we had a hard frost on the Fourth of July this past summer!"

"You don't have a wife?" Longarm had moved up behind the man to look out the window.

"Nah. None of the married fellas stay up here in the winter. The wives have sense enough to call 'em or lead 'em down to warmer temperatures." Rappaporte emptied his mug and glanced at Longarm. "Where's Miss Hathaway?"

"Gonna stay aboard her car."

"You think that's wise?"

"She has her monkeys."

Rappaporte chuffed dryly, set his mug on the counter, grabbed his bottle, which he stuffed down into his coat pocket, bid Longarm adieu and good luck, and headed out into the storm, angling toward the left side of the creek as he trudged through the snow toward Miss Tulip's cabin.

Longarm looked around the darkening depot, then stepped outside, into the passengers' overlaid tracks that were already being obliterated. The wind gusted, and Longarm quickly splayed his hand over his hat crown, to keep it on his head, and squinted into the blowing snow. The wind sounded weird in this canyon—like a crazy man shouting at the tops of his lungs. It was a chilling, echoing caterwauling, and Longarm stared straight up the canyon, into the blowing snow, and felt another icy finger of dread prod his loins.

He stepped off the platform and trudged up the street toward where he could see the tail end of the passengers' group—ghostly dark, jostling figures—slipping quickly away from him. He increased his own pace, the fresh snow feathering up around his knees, his lungs working hard at this altitude, the cold raking his chest like sandpaper.

Walking, he caressed the thumb of the Winchester he carried on his right shoulder, his saddlebags draped over his left, and looked around cautiously for any flickering shadows that might be the killer lurking around the bottom of an outside staircase or poking his head out from behind a rain barrel.

The man—or whatever the killer was—was probably holed up in one of the many cabins that had been abandoned by those who'd left for the winter. He probably had a fire going, and was warming some coffee and whiskey and getting ready to throw a venison steak into a pan. But that cold knife blade continued to nip at Longarm's haunches, and he wasn't taking any chances.

He thought about the killer's hideout. In weather like this, the man was surely holed up in a shelter of some kind. Longarm would find out from Carson or someone else in the Trinity which cabins were occupied by villagers, and he'd look for tracks or wood smoke around those that were supposedly vacant. It was as good a way to track the son of a bitch as any, and it was better than just kicking back, waiting for him to kill again—though night was falling quickly now and Longarm would have to wait till morning.

Maybe the storm would blow itself out by morning, and he'd have the train passengers out of his hair. Then he'd only have the few winter residents of Sully Creek to worry about while he drove the killer to ground.

He shuffled through the snow until he saw the passengers angling onto the Trinity's front porch, the first one pushing through the door. The two saddle tramps Longarm had seen on the train were at the tail end of the group, laughing and festively sharing a bottle. The others were a stove-up old man and woman, a pregnant young woman and her boy and husband—a tall, mustachioed and spade-bearded young man clad in a long, ratty fur coat and a sealskin hat—as well as a couple of whiskey drummers and one stocky, limping gent in miner's garb, though he might also have been an itinerant rail worker. The young man in the long fur coat stepped back and with the little boy—who was around eight or so—held the Trinity's door open for his pregnant wife and the others, who tramped in quickly, futilely stomping snow from their heavy boots on the unshoveled porch.

On the other side of the creek, the stationmaster, Rappaporte, was just now rapping on the door of Miss Tulip.

Presently the door opened and the girl's rawboned, smiling face appeared beneath the antlers, and she frowned with concern as she held the buffalo robe around her shoulders and, with good-natured cajoling, stepped back to order the man "out of that gall-blasted crazy weather this instant!"

They went inside. Longarm looked around. All he could see was blowing snow and the blurred shapes of stores and cabins, hear only the eerily mewling wind and the raucous clanking of shingle chains. Someone had apparently tired of hearing the slamming door and secured it.

Longarm looked at the undertaker/furniture maker's sloping shed and peak-roofed cabin attached to the shed's right side. He should go over and talk to the man about the dead constable and the constable's deputy, but first he'd best go on into the Trinity and make sure Carson wasn't fleecing the stranded train passengers.

And that's just what the saloon/hotel proprietor was doing.

Longarm, stomping in from the porch, got in on the tail end of the ambuscade, with Bill Carson holding his bloody nose while the stove-up old woman in the party, clad in a heavy black coat, black blanket wrapped around her head, and fur boots, pointed a stubby, crooked finger at him: "Shame on you! May you go to hell for such sins! *Himmelshilfe Sie!* Going easy on the price of the rooms so you can stick us for coal!"

She raised the accordion bag in her right hand, as if to smash it again across Carson's face. Longarm rushed forward and clamped his hand down on the old woman's arm before all broke loose.

Chapter 11

"Hold on, ma'am," Longarm admonished the old German woman. "I'm sure you got your reasons, but . . . what's goin' on here, Carson. You and I need to have another chat?"

As the old woman whipped around to scowl at Longarm, hardening her jaws and sparking her black eyes furiously, her old husband held her back from attempting a further assault. Carson held a big hand over his nose, which was bleeding down across his lips, and said in a nasally voice, "The old bitch damn near busted my schnoz, Marshal!"

The tall, bearded gent who'd been playing "horse" to Carson's "rider" laughed as he stoked the potbellied stove.

"I saw the whole thing, Marshal!" Flora called from her table, where she was still playing solitaire, her eyes glassy from drink. "The old lady threw the first punch, but Carson had it comin'! I say you let her do it again if for no other reason than the sawed-off son of a bitch waters down his coffin varnish overmuch . . . as if the strychnine didn't make it damn near undrinkable its own self!"

Longarm was about to order Flora to shut the hell up, when he saw the young pregnant woman, the tall young man in the long fur coat, and the little boy standing on the far side of the room, all three looking as nervous as cats in a roomful of rocking chairs. The young mother, bundled in a long buffalo robe and wearing a sealskin hat, high fur boots, and knitted red mittens, looked more than merely nervous. She was gaunt and pale and wobbly on her feet, no doubt due to the trek through knee-deep snow after a long, herky-jerky train ride.

Longarm felt a rake of anger at Rappaporte and Hollis for not seeing that the woman and her family had been hauled up here in a sleigh. The town likely had plenty of them forted up in sheds and barns. He hadn't thought of it himself, but he had the killer to think about. The passenger's were the trainmen's territory.

Longarm slung his saddlebags over a chairback and walked over to the young family, the little boy—broad-faced, with freckles splashed across his nose and cheeks and large ears—staring up at Longarm's badge as though at the holy rapture.

As the lawman stopped before them, the boy's eyes snapped wide as 'dobe dollars, and standing there in his little wool coat, baggy, patched denims, rubber boots, and stocking cap, he said, "Are you gonna arrest my pa, Sheriff?"

"Clancy!" the young woman admonished.

Longarm chuckled. "Not today, Clancy." To the young woman and the young man, who was pale and sharp-featured behind his coal-black mustache and goatee,

Longarm said, "You three go on upstairs. Take any empty room you find. It'll cost you fifty cents, if you have it, but there'll be no charge for the coal and hot water for a bath that Carson here'll be hauling up shortly." Over his shoulder, he gave Carson a sharp, commanding look.

Smiling with relief, the young man bent his knees as he reached down for the bulging leather trunks on the floor to each side of him. "Thank you, sir. We'll do that. Come, now, Clancy. It's not polite to gawk!"

The young man ushered the young woman to the rear of the room and around the bar, and Clancy followed, turning full around to keep his eyes on Longarm's badge. When the three were on the stairs, heading up into the shadows, the young father grunting under the weight of the two steamer trunks, Longarm turned back to the rest of the room that had fallen silent, waiting to hear what he had to say next. Carson was holding a handkerchief to his broad beak and regarding the severe-looking old woman cautiously.

"At ease, ma'am," Longarm said. "I believe he got the message."

The old German woman gave a "Harumph!" and showed Carson her bony fist once more while her stooped old husband, who wore a silver walrus mustache and had a patch over one eye, clucked to her reprovingly.

To all the passengers sort of gathered around the lawman expectantly, Longarm said, "Mr. Carson wants everyone to feel at home until the storm blows out and the tracks have been cleared, and you can all continue your journey . . . those of you who aren't at the end of the line, that is. Rooms are fifty cents apiece, or you can sack out down here for free. Understandably, he'll be charging you for food and hooch. If he tries to charge for coal, just let the the missus here know, and I got a feelin' he'll have another change of heart."

The old woman showed her proud, devilish, gap-toothed grin to Longarm. Carson cursed under his breath and favored the lawman with a rabid glare.

"Heard the constable was killed here in Sully Creek," said one of the two saddle tramps, saddlebags draped over his shoulder. He carried a Sharps carbine from a sling around his neck. He wore a quilted deerskin coat, and his battered Stetson was tied to his head with a green scarf. "That why you're here, Marshal?"

"That's right."

"I got me a purty good sniffer, and what I'm purty damn sure I smelled in the depot station was blood. Wasn't beef blood, neither."

Longarm glowered back at the man. The first saddle tramp's partner, who wore his hair in two short hide-wrapped braids, gave a knowing grin that was as gap-toothed as the old lady's.

One of the two drummers—a freckle-faced man with one blue and one brown eye—cleared his throat tentatively as he turned to Longarm. "The . . . uh . . . lawmen's killer is . . . still around?"

"I don't know," Longarm grunted. Of course, the villagers here at the Trinity would have told the passengers about the killings sooner or later, but he'd hoped later rather than sooner. Just one person losing his head could turn the whole lot into addled fools, and he had enough on his mind without throwing mass hysteria into the mix. "That's what I'm here to find out. Nothin' for you folks to worry about. Why don't you belly up to the bar and help Carson pay for his coal? Likely he'll be getting around to supper soon."

Grumbling and looking around at each other skeptically, the men shifted their gear on their shoulders or unloaded it onto chairs or beneath tables, and clomped across the saloon to the bar, as did Carson, who tipped his head back, giving his nose a couple more gingerly swipes with his handkerchief.

The old German woman informed her husband that she was heading upstairs to a warm bed and ordered him to bring her a bottle of brandy. "Not anything that son of a bitch brews, though, Oscar!"

She sniffed and, grabbing her two ragged carpetbags, limped heavily upstairs.

Longarm was contemplating shoving up to the bar, as well—a stiff drink might knock the chill out of his bones—when the door opened behind him. He swung around to see the conductor, Avril Hollis, stomp through the door, carrying a worn carpetbag by a shoulder strap. His round spectacles instantly fogged. As he closed the door behind him, Longarm said, "Where's Tibbs?"

Hollis doffed his leather-billed watch cap and tossed it onto a chair. "Thought he came with you. I was securing the cars, though Miss Hathaway's men wouldn't let me lock the parlor car. They assured me they'd keep track of how much they drank and ate . . ." As the conductor removed his foggy, snowy spectacles, he frowned at Longarm. "What's the matter?"

The federal lawman had moved to the window right of the front door and was staring into the storm, brown brows furled with consternation. "Tibbs."

"Eugene can take care of himself. He used to fight In-juns up in Wyoming, and he was married to a redhead. Ha!"

Longarm glanced at the chair on which he'd deposited his saddlebags and war sack. "Watch my possibles."

"Where you goin'? It's gettin' dark out there, Custis, and colder'n a witch's pussy!"

Longarm opened the door, ducking into a blast of snow and brittle wind, and headed outside, the wind nearly ripping the door out of his hand and slamming it to kindling sticks against the frame. He closed it carefully then raised his coat collar, hefted his rifle, and tramped through the snow-covered porch, down the steps, and out into the ever-darkening street.

He could see the winding black creek before him, and only a shadowy blur of the buildings beyond it and to each side of him, and little else. If he was going to find Tibbs, he'd have to run right up on the engineer.

He shouted, "Tibbs!" And immediately felt foolish. The moaning, howling wind that sounded now like a hundred maniacs screaming in swirling circles around him, rendered the call nearly silent to even himself.

He pulled his hat brim low and, wincing against old Jack Frost's rabid chomping at his ears, slogged through the quickly disappearing tracks of the passengers as he headed back in the direction from which he'd just come. On the other side of the creek, to his right, a wan light shone in the cabin of Miss Tulip, and he wished for a moment he'd taken the girl up on her offer. He didn't make a habit of sleeping with whores, as he'd just never really needed to pay for his loving, but on a night like tonight the plain though comely blonde would have made for soft snuggling in a warm bed.

The stationhouse door was locked.

Longarm peered through the glass but was able to see little but shadows and the dark shapes of benches. He'd thought maybe Tibbs had decided to remain in the station, as the engineer was a taciturn loner, born for long, solitary hours in a locomotive, but if he were here, a lamp would be lit, and there'd be a fire in the wood stove. The depot was cold and dark.

Longarm called for the man again, and his shout sounded louder here under the station's sheltering overhang, but the only response was the wind and the ticking, sifting snow pelting his hat and falling around his boots.

Cursing, feeling the cold in his toes and working like sandpaper at his ears—he had a scarf, which Cynthia Larimer had given him, in his war bag; why hadn't he put it on?—walked around the end of the depot building, skirting the chopping block and the snow-covered blood of Foyle Goody, to the train.

He was angling toward the hulking black locomotive, when he stopped suddenly.

Something was on the ground between the tender car and the engine, sort of slumped back against the tender car's front wheel. Longarm felt ice spurt through his veins. He hurried forward, blinking against the snow sticking to his lashes, then stopped and looked down.

The back of Tibbs's head rested against the tender car's wheel. His arms were thrown out to his sides, one knee jutting outward, the other leg stretching straight out across the rocky rail bed. The man's eyes were open, and they seemed to be lit with an inner light.

The bottom of his heavy buckskin mackinaw was dark. Blood dark. There was a grisly gash through the coat, over the engineer's bulging belly.

Again, ice jetted in Longarm's veins, and feeling the prickling of a million needles along his spine, he swung around, aiming the rifle straight out in front of him.

Nothing but snow and the dark town beyond growing darker as the stormy night descended. To his right were the hulking black masses of the depot and the rest of the train. Between the train and the depot building, the snow shown like buttermilk.

No movement but the snow that bounced off the sides of the train cars.

Turning back to the engineer, Longarm knelt, removed his glove from his left hand, and dipped a finger into the oily blood at Tibbs's middle. Still warm. Longarm wiped the blood on the man's duck trousers, slipped on the glove, and looked around.

Scuffed tracks led straight out away from Tibbs's slumped body toward the village nestled deep in the stormy canyon.

Rage burned through Longarm, warming him from his toes to the tips of his near-frozen ears. He gritted his teeth and hardened his jaws. "Come on out, you son of a bitch!" He loudly racked a shell into the Winchester's chamber. "Come on out here and face me, you murderin' coward!"

The only reply was the demonically howling wind.

His heart hammering with raw fury liberally laced with frustration, he moved out away from the train and circled the depot station twice. Sidestepping through the snow, he moved cautiously, holding the cocked rifle straight out in front of him.

He'd thought the killer might have circled around him, maybe intending to bury a knife in his back. The man had been here recently, had maybe even run off when he'd seen Longarm heading for the depot.

But finding no one, Longarm followed the man's tracks toward the edge of the village, where they faded quickly until Longarm was walking through virgin snow that was quickly purpling with night shadows and staring at the blurred outlines of a village under siege by not only a savage storm but a maniacal killer.

Chapter 12

Longarm squeezed his rifle in both hands as he stared at the two lines of buildings facing each other on both sides of the darkly meandering stream. Obscured by gauzy curtains of buffeting snow, the village would soon be concealed completely by the night tumbling down from the soupy gray ridges.

It was charcoal dusk now. In a half hour, the village would be as black as the inside of a glove. The killer would be invisible. But lantern light would show him the occupied shacks . . . and the Trinity Saloon filled with innocent villagers and train passengers.

Likely, more people would die unless Longarm managed to run him to ground soon, in spite of thickening darkness.

The lawman thought of Janice Hathaway, and he turned to stare back past the depot building, on the southern flank of which he could barely make out the squat, rectangular box of the actress's private car. Her shades were drawn, but wan light pushed out along their edges, and he could see a thin, gray wash of smoke blowing up from the car's chimney pipe before the wind obliterated it.

Longarm wheeled and trudged back through the ever-deepening snow. He walked around the left side of the depot, through snow-mounded brush, and up onto the vestibule of the actress's car. He pounded the door, and yelled above the wind, "It's Longarm! Open up!"

There was the soft thud of footsteps. The door opened, and Janice stood facing him in one of her spectacular dresses and with a heavy black-and-velvet-pink cloak thrown haphazardly about her shoulders. Her jeweled necklace and earrings sparkled in the light of the crystal chandeliers and subtly tinted lamp chimneys.

"Why, Custis—you look like you've seen a ghost!" She drew the door wide and beckoned him inside. "You're half froze!"

Longarm stomped inside, not caring that he brought a half-bushel of snow in on his boots and trouser cuffs and which he deposited on her frilly, flower-patterned, wine-red rug. He closed the door quickly and turned to the four brutes flanking her, all sitting around a table in brocade-upholstered chairs, smoking and playing cards, whiskey goblets before them. There was an empty chair at their table, and on the table before the chair was a half-filled wineglass. The five of them, including Janice, had a poker game going while the killer was likely sniffing around their car.

Longarm scowled at the men who regarded him with incredulity in their arched or wrinkled brows. "Why'd you let her answer the door?"

Drake, the blond ape with the scarred face to which

Longarm had added his own mark, flushed. "She wanted to."

Janice said, "You did halloo-the-camp, Custis. I knew I wasn't giving entrance to a savage killer." She fingered her necklace. "Worried about me?"

"Stow it. I just found the engineer dead, his guts leaking out a fist-sized hole in his belly."

"Oh, dear!" Janice gasped, bringing her hands to her face.

"Good work, Longarm," mocked Louis around the cigar in his teeth, his gray eyes sharp. "Thought it was your job to bring peace and justice to Sully Creek. How many's the crazy bastard gonna—?"

"Shut up, Louis!" Janice turned to Longarm. "We've seen no sign of the killer here, Marshal. Why don't you come and get warm. Your cheeks are white. You're frostbit."

"I'm gonna be more frostbit before the night's over." Longarm ran his sleeve across his brows to which melting snow clung. "I just came to see if you'd seen or heard anything. Since you haven't, I'll be runnin' along." He regarded the four beefy cardplayers severely. "Make sure at least one of you is up and awake—and I mean bright-eyed and bushy-tailed—all night. The kill-crazy son of a bitch is likely to strike again, and I'd bet credits to navy beans he'd love to have a notch for a famous actress in his knife handle."

"Custis, must you be so uncouth? You're frightening me."

"It's about time."

A smile pulled at her mouth though it couldn't edge

the apprehension from her large, brown eyes. "You are worried about me." She touched his forearm. "Why don't you stay here and protect me yourself? And keep me warm?"

Longarm flushed with embarrassment as the four thugs scowled at him jealously.

"He's got a job to do, Miss Hathaway," Drake said, glaring at Longarm while rolling his cigar between his lips. "Got him a killer to rundown. Ain't sure he's up to it."

Janice arched a brow at the federal lawman, who stood regarding her thugs from beneath angrily mantled brows. "Do you want me to send out some of my boys?" she offered. "They could help you scour the town, run the killer off or run him down." She glanced at the sullen thug to her right, whose big, jade ring flashed on his sausagelike pinky finger. "Reynolds was once a deputy sheriff, weren't you, Reynolds?"

Longarm suppressed his anger and frustration and considered the offer for about two seconds. These fellas were all swollen muscles and bluster. They'd serve the lawman better here in the railcar, protecting the actress. Out in the maniac-haunted storm, they'd be prime quarry.

Longarm shook his head. "No one leave the car. And keep the doors locked up tighter'n a nun's corset."

With that, he shouldered his rifle and went out.

He tramped down a couple of the village's side streets, though in this weather it was hard to tell the side streets from alleys.

He found no tracks or any sign of the killer. What he did find on the south side of the town, amongst the stables, privies, and stock pens arranged willy-nilly around nearly buried cedars and boulders and slashing ravines, was a lone cabin with a light on.

He knocked on the door, which was answered by a shaggy-headed, round-shouldered man who was apparently mute. Clad in buckskins and a stocking cap, a bib beard dangling over his bulging paunch, he smelled like something wild. So wild, in fact, that Longarm's eyes nearly watered against the fetor. The mute said nothing in response to the lawman's warnings about the killer.

After listening closely, politely to the strange lawman, he merely gave a bearlike grunt, nodded, closed the door, and locked it with a wooden rasp of the locking bar.

Longarm wasn't overly suspicious of the gent. Most mountain towns had their hermits. While this man was maybe powerful enough to have killed Foyle Goody and cut his head off, he likely wasn't the killer. If he were, he wouldn't have answered the knock on his door so readily, and to Longarm's seasoned sniffer, he just didn't smell like a cutthroat. He smelled like a man who just wanted to be left alone and likely had been for many years.

Besides, there were no tracks in the snow around his cabin, however faint. No tracks around the other cabins out this way, either, and no further lights bespeaking habitation.

Where in the hell was the killer holed up? He had to have a fire going. Not necessarily a lamp, but without a fire he'd freeze to death . . .

Curling his aching toes in his boots to get some blood flowing, he made his way to the north side of town and, on a cursory inspection made nearly impossible by the

blowing snow and brutally falling temperatures, found
only three occupied cabins—Miss Tulip's place and two
others that were also home to sporting girls. Miss Wilomena and Miss Rae were both entertaining men from
the Trinity—a drummer from the train and the tall man,
Sylvus, who doubled as Carson's "horse," respectively.

Longarm found Miss Tulip still entertaining Rappaporte in front of a hot fire, but the two came up from
love's embrace long enough to exclaim at the news of
Tibbs's demise and to assure Longarm they'd keep the
cabin door locked and wouldn't venture outside. Rappaporte didn't sound as though he'd given much thought to
surfacing from the girl's cabin, anyway. He looked damn
cozy in there, all but his head buried under the girl's
heavy quilts and robes, a complacent set to his mustached mouth.

When Miss Tulip had closed her cabin door, dropped
the locking bar into its iron brackets, and tiptoed back to
bed and the waiting Sully Creek mayor and stationmaster, Longarm tramped back to the Trinity. Several men,
including Carson, whose nose was swollen, were waiting by the window. All were wielding rifles or had pistols tucked behind the waistbands of their pants. Others
sat around the ticking stove or played poker at tables in
the stove's general vicinity, while a drummer and the two
saddle tramps stood drinking with a moody, desultory air
at the bar.

By the sharp, concerned looks in their eyes, the train
passengers had been well briefed on the trouble here in
Sully Creek. The two women passengers, the German
and the pregnant mother, were upstairs. The mannish Flora
sat where she'd been sitting before. The young husband

and father was playing cards with a couple of drummers, and he regarded Longarm curiously, obviously a timid, shy young man.

Avril Hollis stood with his back to the stove, a soapy beer mug in his brown fist. "You find Tibbs?"

"Yep." Longarm set his rifle on a table near the door, hammered snow from his hat, and dropped it onto the rifle. "Gutted like a damn fish."

"What?"

"You heard me."

A low roar of exclamation rose from the men in various clumps around the room. Carson, who had an old Remington .44-40 sticking up from behind his waistband, jutted his sharp nose at Longarm. "The killer's still out there?"

"Yep." Longarm bit off his gloves and shrugged out of his coat. "What do you know about the mute in the cabin over yonder?"

"Herman Waverly," Carson said. "He's touched but he's no killer." He turned a haunted look to the window. "I'll be damned . . ."

Longarm draped his coat over a chairback, hitched his cartridge belt high on his hips, and dug a cheroot from his shirt pocket, confronting the room and all faces now regarding him warily and with deep consternation. "No one venture outside tonight. In fact, no one venture outside till I give the say-so."

"What about wood?" one of the locals asked from near the stove. "It's stacked out back."

"Let Carson get it," quipped Scotty, the big man with the bald, bullet-shaped head. He was playing cribbage with Flora.

"When we need more wood or coal, several of you'll fetch it, and I'll stand guard with the Winchester. We'll bring in enough to last the night."

"What about tomorrow, there, Marshal?" asked Flora, her voice buoyant with drink. "We gonna be stuck in here the rest of the winter?"

"Yeah," said the saddle tramp with the braided hair and a mulish look. He and his partner had their backs to the bar, and they both looked off their feed. "We just gonna cower in here till the first crocus blooms? I say we all head out there, scour the damn town, and root that crazy bastard out of his hole and hang him from the nearest damn tree!"

Several other men around the room agreed, nodding.

"If it comes to that," Longarm said, lighting his cheroot and blowing smoke out the side of his mouth, "I'll deputize a couple of you, and we'll go out there and root him out in an orderly fashion. But only when and if I say it comes to that. Otherwise, you all are gonna stay put and keep yourselves on a short leash. And you'll refrain from ruffling my feathers. They're already kinda ruffled, to tell the truth, and my toes are cold. I will take exactly no bullshit from any of you, and, to a man . . . and woman . . . you'll follow my orders."

He waved out the match, tossed it onto the table he'd claimed for himself, and sent a hard look the length of the room, past the grinning Flora, to the two owl-eyed saddle tramps. "Everyone understand, or do I need to chew it finer?"

Silence. Someone grumbled under his breath. Burning wood dropped in the stove with a soft, crunching thump.

The two saddle tramps held Longarm's stare, then, sharing moody glances, turned to slump against the bar.

Longarm told Carson to bring him a mug of beer and a bottle—he knew the futility in asking for Maryland rye this far out in the rocks—then dropped into a chair, sliding his gear aside with a forearm. Carson brought the drink, his eyes darting around nervously after the lawman's harangue, and set the shot and the glass carefully on the table. Rubbing his hands on his pants, he said, "You want me to fetch some stew, Marshal Long? I got a big pot full and so far only Mrs. Becker and the boy, Clancy, have eaten of it. I reckon the others're a might distracted, don't ya know?"

"Bring me the stew and some bread, and if you got any cheroots back there, I'll take those, too. Mine're soggy."

"Right away!"

As the diminutive barman headed toward the rear of the room, Flora swatted his ass, and Carson yelped with a start. "Bring me some, too, Shorty, then get over here and warm my tired old bones!" She threw back her shot and gave Longarm a meaningful look as she set the glass back down on the table. "Got a feelin' this night's gonna git cold and grim."

She was right. The night got cold and grim.

After the others had a bowl of Carson's stew, and Longarm, the barman, Scotty, and the quiet young father had fetched in enough coal and wood to last till morning, they all sat around in moody silence, drinking and playing cards, tipping their heads and cocking their ears every time the wind-racked walls creaked overloud or a pine knot popped in the potbellied stove.

Longarm got coaxed into a game of two-hand stud with Flora. Then, after the mannish woman fell asleep on the floor near the fire, head propped on a grain sack, Longarm kicked back in his own chair and folded his arms on his chest.

Thump! Thump! Thump!

He lifted his chin from his chest with a start, blinking his sleepy eyes and looking around. A few of the others stirred in the near-dark saloon hall.

Longarm's right hand drifted across his belly toward his pistol. "What the hell . . . ?"

Thump! Thump! Thump!

Longarm turned to the door behind which rose the faint, pinched voice of a distressed female. "Custis! Oh, God—let me *in*!"

Longarm sprang to his feet and opened the door. The snowy, near-frozen package of Janice Hathaway slumped into his arms.

Chapter 13

"Janice!" Longarm stooped to snake his arms under the girl clothed in an ankle-length, snow-basted mink coat, then hefted her high against his chest as he kicked the door closed. "What in the hell're you doin', girl? I told you to stay put!"

She sobbed. "Oh, Custis—it was awful!"

"What was awful?" He looked around for a place to put the chilled, wet bundle in his arms.

Flora and the men in the room had all gained their feet, anxious looks on their sleep-craggy faces. Some held pistols; others, rifles. Flora whipped her blanket up off the floor in front of the stove, and pointed in the general direction of the feed sack she'd used as a pillow. "Put her down there, Marshal!"

Bill Carson stood regarding Longarm's furry package like a little boy inspecting his newborn baby sister, only the saloonkeeper held a double-bore shotgun in his hands. "What the hell's that?"

"It's a girl, you fuckin' idiot." Longarm, spying no place more fitting than the floor near the fire, carried

Janice through the small, hushed crowd that had gathered to get a look at what the storm had blown in and slowly bent his knees to lower the woman to the floor.

Flora knelt on Janice's other side. "We best get that coat off of her, get her warm."

Longarm and Janice both worked on the coat's large, fancy buttons. Flora eased the girl to a sitting position, and they worked the coat off the girl's shoulders and down her arms. She hadn't been wearing mittens or gloves, and her hands, Longarm felt, were cold as stones.

"Christ, you're damn froze solid, girl."

"Oh . . . Custis . . . it was . . . it was . . ."

Gentling her back down against the floor, Longarm grabbed Flora's blanket and laid it over the actress, who stared up at him with terrified eyes, the snow on her lashes and brows just beginning to melt. Her cheeks were red, her lips blue, and she shivered as though lightning struck.

"Easy, now," Longarm said, tucking the blanket tight against her body. "Where are your men? Can you tell me? Are they out there, too?"

Janice nodded, tried to speak, stopped, licked her lips, and tried again. "We heard sounds. Laughing, howling sounds." She took a deep breath, swallowed, and seemed to make an effort to quell her shaking. Lifting her arms above the blanket, she closed her hands around the lapels of Longarm's frock coat. "At first we thought it was the wind, Custis. Louis went out to investigate."

More tears formed in her eyes, and dribbled down her bright red cheeks that Longarm caressed with his thumbs, trying to get the blood flowing. Meanwhile, Flora was behind him, taking the actress's socks off. She must have run out in her shoes, Longarm realized, and lost them in the snow. Or maybe in her panic she'd left the car without them.

As Flora tried to rub some circulation back into the girl's brick-red feet, Longarm looked down into her horror-bright eyes again. "Okay, I'm with you so far, Janice. Louis went out to investigate some noises."

"And never came back!" Janice fairly shrieked, sniffing and swallowing and bunching Longarm's coat lapels in her small, red fists. "And one by one the others went out . . . and didn't return. Until I was there all alone." Her voice pinched down until it was just barely audible, and she sobbed, tears running as though a pump had been primed inside her. "And then . . . the face . . . in my window . . . The horrible, grinning face . . . and the horrible *howling* . . . !"

"You saw him?"

"Yes! He was in my window! Over my bed. And then he had a knife in his teeth, and I was going mad with fear and before I knew what I was doing I was getting into my coat and running outside!"

Her voice broke off and she released Longarm's coat, sagging back against the feed sack pillow, bawling.

"Can you tell me what he looked like?"

"He looked like a *savage!*"

Longarm turned to Flora, who was rubbing the girl's bare right foot hard. "Take care of her Flora. I'm gonna go—"

He stopped as Janice clawed at his arm, pulled him back down to her.

"He really is a maniac, Custis. A wretched, ugly, howling maniac!"

Longarm gently pressed her back down to the floor. "Easy, easy. How'd you get away from him?"

"I ran and . . . suddenly I realized he wasn't behind me anymore. I could hear him howling, but gradually the howling died and then I was just running in the wind and the snow, screaming for *you*!"

Longarm shoved his face down close to hers, brushed her tangled hair back from her pale temples. "You found me, and now you're safe. You rest easy and get warm. Flora here's gonna take care of you while I go out and see what I can see."

Longarm stood as Flora began working on Janice's other foot.

"Don't go out there, Custis," Janice pleaded weakly. "He's purely crazy. A demon. I don't think . . . he's even human . . ."

"Shush, now, missy," Flora cooed to the actress. "You just rest." She turned to Bill and said angrily, "Well, don't just stand there gawkin', you sawed-off bastard. Heat some water! I'm gonna give this poor girl a good hot bath."

Longarm pushed past the men standing around gawking at the actress and grabbed his coat off the table he'd been sitting at. He shrugged into it, donned his hat and gloves—no time for the scarf—and picked up his Winchester. Racking a live round into the chamber, he took a quick look out the window left of the door, holding a hand up to block the light of the few guttering lamps behind him.

Seeing little but slanting snow, he turned to the half dozen men, including the big, bald hombre, Scotty, now regarding him skeptically.

"Lock this behind me."

Scotty strode toward him. He moved like a boxer—big but graceful, sort of rolling his shoulders and clenching his fists. His hobnailed boots clomped loudly on the saloon's wooden floor.

"Want a hand?" The big gent's acrimony had leached out of his eyes. "I was a shotgunner on a stagecoach for a few years, and I've guarded mine shipments. Know my way around a gun—and a knife, comes to that."

"'Preciate the offer, but that killer's probably gone back to his hole by now. I'm just gonna have a quick look around." Longarm turned to the door, then glanced back at Scotty regarding him grimly. "I might take you up on that offer tomorrow, though."

"It'll stand."

Longarm opened the door and hurled himself quickly outside, like a ship's captain bulling out from the wheelhouse of a storm-tossed schooner, and kicked the door closed behind him. He heard the click as Scotty locked it.

Stepping to the left of the door and window, he squinted against the pelting snow, instantly feeling the cold chewing at his cheeks and ear tips, nipping at his toes. He could see in detail only a dozen or so feet in front of him. On the other side of the creek, which he couldn't see at all, the light of Miss Tulip's cabin shone dully, nearly winking out with each sporadic wind gust.

The wind howled like a pack of giant wolves. It thrashed a shingle hanging by chains over the porch's front steps announcing dime whiskey, nickel beer, and free sandwiches. It made the roof joists creak and sigh.

Longarm lifted his left leg over the porch rail and dropped to the ground between the hotel/saloon and the

next business building that hulked darkly several yards
to his left. The deep snow cushioned his landing. Putting
his back to the saloon's wall, he looked around the gap,
shuttling his gaze from the building's rear to the front.

He hadn't returned his gaze to the street before he
jerked it back toward the rear of Carson's place, his heart
quickening.

He'd spied movement—a shadow just a tad darker
than the night's stormy darkness flitting from the rear of
the hotel/saloon to the rear of the building just beyond.

Pushing off the wall, Longarm shambled as fast as he
could through the deep drift that had piled up in the gap,
to the rear corner of the next building. Lifting his rifle in
both hands, he edged a look around behind the place.

The shadow was jerking, dwindling into the dark,
snowy distance.

A man running away from him.

"Hold it!" Longarm shouted against the wind.

Twenty yards away, a pinprick of light flashed. The
gun's report was barely louder than a distant twig snap-
ping. The bullet whispered past Longarm's left ear.

Gritting his teeth, he smashed the Winchester's butt
against his right shoulder and fired twice, levering quickly,
the rifle leaping in his hands, but the reports sounding
like small-caliber pistol shots in the storm.

Seating another shell in the Winchester's breech, Longarm shuffled farther into the gap behind the building on
his right, in case the killer reckoned on the flash of Longarm's rifle, and dropped a knee into the deep snow,
keeping the Winchester aimed straight out from his right
shoulder.

Another flash from farther away than the first—also

lower and slightly right. Longarm could barely hear the pistol's pop but he heard the nasty thump of the bullet tearing into some snow-buried rubble piled against the building's rear wall.

Aiming at the spot where he'd seen the second gun flash, Longarm squeezed the Winchester's trigger, levered, fired, then levered and fired again. As he ejected the last spent cartridge, he heaved himself up out of the snow and ran forward, his heart hammering eagerly, his knees pumping high. He couldn't see the shadow now, but when he'd run a good fifty yards, he came to another gap between buildings, and, looking down, saw fresh, ragged tracks in the knee-deep powder.

They led into the gap. They were spaced several feet apart. The killer was running.

Longarm had taken two long strides when a shadow moved before him, jutting up from behind some rubble on his right. There was a flash of two angry eyes and gritted white teeth. Then he saw the board arcing toward him, held taut in two mittened hands, and he'd barely gotten his rifle raised defensively before the board smashed into his right forearm and then landed a glancing blow across his temple.

Losing his rifle, Longarm twisted around and left and hit the snow on his belly.

A man's tooth-gnashing yowl rose above that of the storm.

Longarm rolled left just as a pistol popped. He glimpsed the flash in the corner of his left eye. As he scrambled around for the rifle but was unable to feel it in the cold, cottony snow, he heard a dull metallic click—like that of a misfired pistol.

Pushing up on his elbows, he saw a bulky figure before him—heavy fur coat and deerskin hat with earflaps—angrily toss his pistol aside and lift a knife from a wide belt sheath jutting up from behind the shaggy coat.

The dark, bulky figure moved toward Longarm, who heard the howl again but only briefly, as it stopped abruptly when Longarm kicked his right boot up savagely from the ground and buried the square toe in the howling killer's crotch.

The figure bent forward, bringing both hands, including that holding the knife, over his oysters. Longarm, digging desperately under his coat for his pistol, heard him groan. The killer staggered back, and again Longarm heard the howl as the man raised the big knife that flashed in the ambient snow light.

Longarm closed his right hand around the smooth walnut grips of his Colt, but as he slid the gun from the holster, it got tangled in the sheepskin lining. The maniac seemed to realize Longarm's predicament. He howled again, adding laughter to the crazed exultation and filling Longarm's belly with little creepy-crawlies of dread, and then the stocky, fur-clad hombre flipped the knife so that he held it with the savagely upcurved tip pointed down.

He bounded off his heels and dove toward Longarm, cocking his arm for a killing stab to the lawman's neck.

Longarm flung his left hand straight up and grabbed the killer's right wrist as the man slammed down on top of him. He gripped the wrist so that the point of the knife was just beginning to tickle the skin over his jugular vein. Smelling the man's unwashed fetor and the rancid aroma of his coat, hearing his grunting mewling beneath the lashing wind and pelting snow, he jerked his

.44-40 free of his coat and rammed the barrel against the man's ribs.

The man stopped squirming and his eyes snapped wide beneath cinnamon brows.

He stared into Longarm's own eyes, his lips stretched back from long, yellow, tobacco-stained teeth, the right front one showing a long, jagged hairline fracture. He continued to press the knife down toward Longarm's throat, the point now feeling like a bee sting.

Longarm gritted his teeth, rammed the .44's barrel harder against the man's ribs and, glaring into the man's exasperated blue eyes, squeezed the trigger.

The killer jerked.

His brows beetled.

Longarm squeezed the double-action's trigger again, and again the man jerked. His eyes began to glaze and gain a faintly beseeching cast.

His knife arm slackened but not quickly enough for Longarm, who pumped one more round into the man's ribs, shredding his heart.

The maniac released the knife. It bounced off Longarm's shoulder and tumbled into the snow. Longarm grabbed the man's collar with his left hand and flung his spasming carcass into the snow, as well.

Longarm lay back in the drift, catching his breath, then gave a grunt that the wind drowned as he heaved up onto his left elbow and hip, aiming his pistol at the killer's quivering carcass, the man's mouth working and his eyes blinking rapidly as a thick gob of blood dribbled down over his thick, cracked lower lip.

"There you go, you bastard."

Longarm scrambled up out of the snow and grabbed

his hat, which he'd lost when he'd fallen. He stared down at the killer, and the killer stared up at him from his cocoon of fur and snow. The man's face slackened, losing all expression, until his stocky, fur-clad frame ceased moving. When the man's eyes rolled slightly back into his head, and he was dead, Longarm swiped his left wrist at his forehead that was just now beginning to burn and dribble blood into his eye.

The howling maniac had come within a couple of inches of cleaning his clock.

Dead now, though. He was probably just now getting a nice, warm welcome from Ole Scratch, maybe receiving a couple of painful pokes to the ass with the devil's three-tined fork.

Longarm scrubbed snow across his forehead, holstered his pistol, and tramped back through the snow to the saloon's front door and inside.

"Christ, what happened to you?" one of the men asked. They were sitting at tables, drinking and playing cards again, too anxious to sleep.

"I'll be damned if I didn't run into that bastard." Longarm peeled off his gloves, tossed them onto the floor near the stove, then shrugged out of his coat.

They all just stared at him, waiting.

Longarm draped his coat over his chairback, then sagged down into the chair and splashed whiskey into his empty beer schooner, filling it half full. "He's dead."

He tipped the schooner back.

Chapter 14

Longarm finished his drink and, while the others cele-
brated, went upstairs to check on Janice Hathaway.

Apparently, Flora had helped her to one of the rooms
after ordering the two saddle tramps to haul their gear
into one already occupied by a couple of drummers, and
then rode roughshod over Bill Carson, ordering him up
and down the stairs with alternating buckets of hot and
cold water, sweet-smelling soap, plenty of towels, and a
bottle of brandy.

In the rooms off the second-story hall, a few snores
resounded. Someone—it sounded like the German
woman—was chuckling. Saddlebags draped over his left
shoulder, his rifle in his right hand, and a cheroot smoldering between his teeth, Longarm knocked on the door
behind which he could hear water splashing and Flora's
soothing voice.

Suddenly, Flora's voice lost its soothing. "Bill, I told
you we got all the water we need. Scram! You're just
wantin' a look at this girl's purty tits!"

"It's Longarm." Puffing his cigar, he opened the door and stepped inside.

Janice sat in a fancy copper tub, facing Longarm and bending forward as Flora knelt behind her, scrubbing her back with a sponge. The actress's knees were raised to her chest, but Longarm could still see a good portion of her soapy breasts. Her hair was tied in a loose braid behind her head, and as her eyes found the tall lawman entering her small, humble room, they grew large with relief.

"Oh, Custis—thank God you're back!"

Flora wasn't half so relieved. Over Janice's pretty head, a loosely rolled quirley hanging from a corner of her thin-lipped mouth, the coarse-featured she-male scowled and said, "Mind your manners, lawdog! Can't you see a lady's gettin' a bath?"

Longarm grinned around his cigar—feeling a twinge of lust but also relief that the actress had come around and was looking as healthy and lovely as ever. "I see that."

"Git outta here, Longarm, you lusty dog!"

Janice turned her head to one side. "It's all right, Flora. Custis and I are . . . friends. Would you please excuse us?"

Flora shuttled an annoyed scowl between them both. "Huh?"

"Thank you so much for your ministrations," Janice said, reaching up to pat the hand that Flora had clamped over Janice's shoulder.

"Ah, shit." Flora dropped the sponge in the water between Janice's legs and rose, taking a deep drag from her quirley. Blowing smoke at the low ceiling and peeling her sleeves down her tan, corded arms, she regarded

Longarm with barely concealed disdain. "You get the bastard?"

"Yep."

Janice's eyes snapped wide. "What? He's dead, Custis? Are you sure?"

"Unless he's got an ironclad heart, he's dead as a side of cured beef. I'll drag him inside in the morning, so the locals can get a look at him, maybe identify the son of a bitch."

"Well, damn," Flora said, donning her man's felt hat and brushing up close to Longarm to snarl, "I was beginnin' to wonder if you had it in you, lawdog."

With that, she plucked the quirley from between her lips, gave a caustic chuff, and went out. Her boots clomped off down the hall.

Longarm kicked the door closed and turned to Janice. "You all right?"

"Now that you're here. And that . . . that madman is dead." She gave a quiver, then extended a wet arm to him, opening her hand. "Come. Put your things down, and scrub my back."

"Looked to me like Flora was doin' a pretty thorough job," he said, dropped his saddlebags on a chair and leaning his rifle against the room's only dresser, one leg of which was propped on a brick.

"She was very nice," Janice said, smiling.

Longarm took her hand in his, knelt down beside the tub, lifted her hand to his lips, and kissed it. "Sorry about your boys. Not much point in lookin' for 'em till sunup or the weather breaks."

"They're dead, or they would have come back to the car," she said, frowning as Longarm pressed his lips to her hand. "But I don't want to talk about it anymore tonight, Custis. Call me crass, but I want . . . well, you know what I want." She stared at him darkly, lowering her knees slightly to reveal her pink, jutting nipples riding just above the surface of the sudsy water. "I want to forget this horrible night."

Longarm ran his mouth up her long slender arm to her shoulder, then reached around her to cup her breasts in his hands. She groaned and tipped her head back as he nuzzled her neck and nibbled her ears, caressing her firm, perfectly shaped orbs until the nipples raked against his palms like small bullets.

"Take it out," she whispered, twisting around, snaking her arms around his neck, and pressing her lips to his mustached mouth. She pulled her lips away to say in a raspy, sensuous whisper, "Take that big hog out of your pants and let me suck it, Custis. I want to feel it all the way down my throat."

"Your wish . . ."

Longarm stood. His cock was rock hard and throbbing, pushing against his trousers. As he shrugged out of his coat and let it drop to the floor, Janice pressed the heel of her hand against his raging organ.

"Pull it out," she whined, frowned as she stared at the firm mound in his tweed pants. "Pull it out, out, out!"

He unbuttoned his fly as fast as he could with her pressing her hand against it, then opened the top button of his trousers. His swollen cock caused his trousers to sag, and all he had to do was give them a little nudge, and they dropped around his knees. Before he knew it, Janice had frantically shifted around in the tub, splash-

ing water over the sides, until she was on her knees,
digging his cock out of his balbriggans.

When the member finally bobbed free of its confines,
the actress gave a shudder and a long, deep sigh.

He felt her warm breath on his balls, and mini-
explosions of desire rippled through his loins. She wrapped
her hand around his shaft, squeezed, and pumped while
gently massaging and nuzzling his scrotum. Finally, she
looked up at him fatefully, licked her lips, and dropped
her mouth down over his cock, sliding her warm, wet
lips down his length until he felt the head of his throbbing member delightfully pinched by the actress's expanding and contracting throat.

Up and down went her head. Up and down, up and
down, until Longarm was leaning back on his heels and
curling his toes and stretching his lips back from his
teeth in desperate agony.

"Do believe that's enough of that," he croaked, placing his hands on her shoulders and shoving her back
away from him, then, when her mouth had come reluctantly off his near-exploding member, lifted her to a standing position inside the tub.

"I wanted to finish you," she sniffed, running her
fingers over him and pressing her lips to his throat.

"Nope." Longarm shook his head. "We're gonna finish good and proper over yonder in the old mattress
sack. Then we're gonna sleep like spring lambs."

He shuffled back away from the tub, keeping his eyes
on her as he sat on the edge of the bed and kicked off his
boots. Next, he shucked out of his trousers, then his tie,
vest, and shirt. He practically ripped off his balbriggans,

giving them a kick with his right foot and sailing them up high against the room's far wall.

Janice stood in the tub, watching him lustily, her lips slightly parted, her wet breasts rising and falling sharply. Chicken flesh rose across them, and her nipples stood out like ripe cherries. Longarm doubted she was reacting to a chill, for Flora had stoked the coal stove in the corner until the sheet metal was glowing red.

The wind continued to sigh and batter the windows. The walls creaked and the room's single lamp guttered. Snow cascaded over the building as if thrown every few seconds by an enraged giant.

Naked, his member jutting and pitching, Longarm grabbed a towel off a chairback and brought it over to the tub. Janice reached for it, but Longarm snapped it away.

"Uh-uh. I wanna do it."

She leaned forward to rest her wrists on his shoulders. "Dry away, my well-hung lawman."

Longarm dried her slowly, feeling the head of his cock caress her belly button. He tried to pay no attention to it, as he wanted his blood to cool so that when he finally got the delectable actress into bed, he could enjoy her—and her, him—for at least a couple of minutes before he exploded. As tired as he was from the long day, he doubted he'd be good for more than one bout.

Slowly, he ran the towel across the back of her neck, down her arms, her breasts, then her back and the firm, full lobes of her ass, and when he had them dry he massaged them with his hands while she sighed and nibbled his ears.

"All right." He tossed the towel over his shoulder,

stooped down, lifted her out of the tub, and set her on the floor. Taking the towel once more, he knelt down and thoroughly dried her ankles and fine-boned, delicate feet, lingering over her toes.

He tossed the towel aside, looked up to see the light brown fur at her crotch. It glistened faintly, damp.

Wrapping his arms around her, placing his palms against her ass, he leaned forward to nuzzle her love mound.

"Oh!" she groaned. "Oh . . . God, Custis . . . sweet *Jesus!*"

Her groans grew louder as she spread her feet slightly and he flicked his tongue up and down the sweet, petal-like lobes of her womanly flower.

"Ohhh!" she intoned, spreading her feet still farther apart and burying her fists in his hair.

"Oh . . . Christ . . . you do that"—a shiver rippled all through her—"rather well . . ."

When he had her wet and steamy and nearly howling as loudly as the murdering maniac, he picked her up, tossed her onto the bed, and threw himself down on top of her. He spread her legs and pressed his lips to hers, flicking his tongue in and out of her mouth. She groaned and mewled and wrapped her legs around his back, and suddenly he was plunging deep inside her.

He grunted and rose up on his arms and the tips of his toes, burying his fists into the soft mattress on either side of her head. She stared up at him glassy-eyed, as though she'd taken several drags off an opium pipe.

"Oh, gawd." She sighed as he bucked against her once more. "You're killing me, Custis. Oh, Christ almighty, you're absolutely fucking killing me!"

He hammered against her, feeling sweat pop out on his forehead and dribble into his brows. "Want I should stop?"

She dug her heels farther into his rump, her fingers deeper into his bulging biceps. "You do, I'll fucking *kill you!*"

Twelve wonderful, horrific minutes after they'd started, he plunged his hungry staff into her one final time, and they shook together until the bed sounded as though it were coming apart at every joint. It was nearly a minute before Longarm realized someone was pounding on the wall from the room next door.

"I *said* . . . if you two wouldn't *mind*—some o' us are tryin' to get some *sleep* over here!"

It was one of the saddle tramps.

He grunted, "Sorry, feller."

Janice groaned and fell slack as a wet towel against the mattress.

Longarm collapsed on top of her, rolled onto a shoulder, and felt sleep wash over him like a hundred tons of coal dumped from a high ridge.

He woke sensing trouble. It was a slight vibration in the back of his neck and an intermittent drip of hot water in his bowels.

He looked around. The stove huddled dark in its corner. He hadn't gotten up all night to add coal; instead, in his sleep, he'd pulled the heavy quilts and blankets up over his and Janice's naked bodies. Janice lay snuggled against him in a tight ball, head on his shoulder, one hand splayed across his privates. She was as warm as a furnace under the covers.

Faint gray light pushed through the room's single window. Could it already be dawn? He felt as though he'd just finished fucking the delectable actress only five minutes ago.

He tried to reject the idea of getting up—Janice was too warm and the room was too cold—but his trouble sniffer wouldn't stop sniffing, and the little nipping sensations between his shoulder blades wouldn't cease.

He slid out from beneath the slumbering girl. She groaned. He kept the covers on her as he dropped a foot to the icy floor, then pulled his other leg from the bed quietly. Hearing Janice groan once more, then smack her lips, he padded naked to the window. The cold wrapped around him like a giant snow blanket.

Longarm looked out. The skin between his broad, winglike shoulder blades tensed.

"Holy fuckin' shit," he muttered.

He whipped around, heart thudding, and dressed quickly, frantically, noisily.

"Custis, what on earth . . . ?" Janice said, sitting up and rubbing her eyes.

Grabbing his coat and gun belt and stomping into his boots, he ran out.

Chapter 15

Longarm hitched his cartridge belt around his hips, then, using both rails, descended the stairs to the near-dark saloon hall three steps at a time.

He bounded across the hall, glad that all the men had crowded into a couple of rooms upstairs so he didn't have to hopscotch them. There was only Bill Carson just now hauling in a load of wood from a curtained door-way flanking the bar, looking incredulous at the federal badge toter virtually flying toward the saloon's front door.

"What in tarnation . . . ?" Carson wheezed, looking worse for the wear of last night's celebration in honor of the howling maniac's demise.

Ignoring the man, Longarm unlocked the door, fumbled it open, and tore outside. He crossed the snowy porch in a single bound, dropped down the steps in an-other single leap, and ran at a leftward angle across the snow-drifted street to the creek that ran inky dark and silent in the quiet morning under a heavy sky turning from charcoal to gray.

Longarm was only vaguely aware that the wind had

ceased and that only a few grainy flakes threaded the
slightly breezy air in front of his face. He wasn't aware
of anything much at all except the four dark-clad figures
hanging from two low, stout branches of the single, large,
leafless cottonwood growing up from the southern creek
bank. He stopped under the tree, his heart in his throat,
his face a mask of grim shock and exasperation.

A crow cawed angrily.

Longarm switched his gaze from the thug, Louis, to
the blond gent, Drake, hanging from a noose just off the
gray-eyed bodyguard's left shoulder. The crow sat on
Drake's own right shoulder, its pelletlike black eyes staring proprietarily down at Longarm. Drake didn't seem to
appreciate the crow's presence. Judging from the blood
trickling down from the corner of Drake's right eye, the
bird had been pecking away at the eyeball, and Drake's
lips were stretched wide in a frozen grimace, both eyes
large and staring as the body turned gently in the breeze
that made the rope creak faintly.

The crow cawed again and jutted its little, sharp beak
at Longarm.

The lawman slid his gaze left of the bird to see the
other two bodyguards hanging from the other, lower,
shorter branch on the tree's other side. They hung straight
down, unmoving, wearing expressions similar to Drake's.
Reynolds shifted a little to one side, looking grim with
his drooping eyelids and his mouth corners turned down.

All four men were bibbed in thick, frozen blood that
had washed down from the gaping holes in their necks.
It looked like a couple might have been shot, as well, but
Longarm couldn't tell for all the blood. And what did it
matter? The men were not only dead—shit, he'd figured

they were dead—but they'd been hanged out here in front of the saloon sometime after Longarm had killed—or thought he'd killed—the howling maniac.

They hadn't been here last night when he'd left the saloon in pursuit of the killer. At least, he didn't think they'd been here. It had been so snowy, he hadn't been able to see much. The killer wouldn't have had time to hang the men here in the time between his running Janice to ground and Longarm's stepping out to investigate.

The lawman's heart hammered as he wheeled, his .44 in his hand, looking around desperately, expecting to see the killer closing on him, laughing at his own joke. At the same time, Longarm's brows hooded with a deep consternation and befuddlement. He felt the butt of some ghastly practical joke played on him by a demon.

A door latch clicked behind him. He jerked toward the saloon.

Bill Carson stepped out onto the porch, shrugging into a red plaid mackinaw and frowning toward the cottonwood and Longarm. The dawn was so quiet that Longarm heard the diminutive saloon owner clearly though Carson kept his voice pitched low: "What the shit?"

Snow crunched to the right of the saloon, and Longarm swung his gaze and his gun west along the street to see a bearded man in a thigh-length bear coat and wool hat walk out from between the open shed doors of Engel's Fine Furniture and Undertaking. He puffed a briar pipe as he strolled toward Longarm, his knee-high, lace-up boots crunching loudly in the fresh snow, some drifts of which rose to the man's thighs.

"Don't shoot me, Marshal," the undertaker, Mel Engel, said as gray smoke wafted around his head. "Just here to

look over the work some fairy must've left me over-
night."

Engel chuckled grimly.

"You see anyone out here?" Longarm asked the man.

"Hell, no." Engel stopped and, keeping his pipe between his bearded lips, stared up at the tree. "I just crawled
out from under my robes and looked out the window,
saw you out here staring up at the tree." He looked up
and down the street with a guarded expression. "Business
is still boomin', I see. Crazy past few days, that way."

As if on cue, the crow cawed again then, giving a
squawk of frustration, lit from Drake's shoulder to a
higher limb of the tree.

"Can't be." Longarm turned to the gap between the
saloon and a drugstore that was boarded up for the winter. The gap in which he'd left the maniac's dead carcass.

"I thought you killed the son of a bitch," Carson
croaked as Longarm tramped past the saloon's porch
and trudged through the wavelike drift at the mouth of
the gap.

Longarm said nothing.

The storm had likely continued for a couple of hours
after Longarm's tussel with the maniac, but the snow of
the gap was badly mussed, showing signs of several sets
of tracks. Longarm held his cocked .44 at an angle before him as he approached the spot where he'd left the
dead man, as if expecting the man to suddenly rise up
from the snow and shove a knife at him.

But he wasn't there.

Frozen blood patched the ground around the indenta-
tion the maniac's body had left in the snow. The snow

was as rumpled as an unmade bed, and deep, scuffed tracks angled around behind the end of the Trinity. It looked like two sets, but in such deep snow it was impossible to tell for sure.

"Musta winged him."

Longarm turned to see both Carson and Engel standing in the snow about ten feet away, looking grimly down at the trampled, bloody snow.

The lawman looked at Engel, and he knew the answer before he even asked the question but felt compelled to ask it anyway: "You didn't haul him away, did you?"

"Didn't haul nobody away, Marshal. If you left the maniac here, you apparently didn't kill him."

"I killed him." With his eyes, Longarm followed the tracks around the Trinity's rear corner. "Someone came and hauled him off. Someone he was in cahoots with."

"You mean you think there was more than one maniac?" Carson asked.

"I don't know what I mean, but I'll be goddamned if I ain't gonna find out." Keeping his .44 in his gloved right hand, Longarm began following the tracks.

Behind him, Engel said, "You want I should cut them fellas down and put 'em in boxes?"

"No." Longarm glanced back at the two men staring grimly after him. "You two go back inside and stay there. Don't let anyone else out, neither."

Longarm followed the tracks around the Trinity's rear corner. Behind the building, he could see that there were indeed two sets of tracks, and they were deep, as though both men had been burdened by the dead body they'd obviously carried off. Why they'd carried it off, and who they were, Longarm had no idea, just as he didn't know why in the hell they would have hanged the bodies of Janice's four bodyguards.

Or . . . maybe he did know. There wasn't just one maniac. There were three. At least three.

Shit, for all Longarm knew, there was a whole slough of kill-crazy sons o' bitches holed up somewhere in the village or maybe a cave along one of the towering ridges.

Longarm considered returning to the hotel for his rifle, as, in his haste, he'd run off without it. He nixed the idea. He was on the killers' blood scent now and, judging by how gray the sky was and how slowly it was getting light, more bad weather was likely on the way.

The tracks led around the backs of several more businesses, then veered around a small, log barn hunched in the snow, before dropping into a ravine and angling back through dark pines toward the southern ridge. Longarm knew where the body snatchers had gone even before he'd scrambled up the ravine's far wall, slipping and sliding in the deep snow and feeling the icy crystals oozing up his coat sleeves and into his gloves.

It made sense that they'd be holed up in the original part of the village, where neither their wood smoke nor the light of their lanterns would be detected in the main part of the town. From there, they could slip in and out of the main settlement as they pleased, killing and fleeing.

Who were they? Why were they killing pretty much anyone they came in contact with?

Longarm moved carefully through the tall pines and firs whose branches hung heavy under thick snow mantlings, and he looked around thoroughly, wary of an ambush. The only sounds were the calls of occasional crows, blackbirds, and mountain chickadees. Gradually, the snow began falling more thickly, ticking off the brim of Long-arm's hat.

Shit, here we go again, he thought. More bad weather.

In several places he lost the tracks of the two killers whom he assumed had carried off their maniacal partner, and as he approached the old village nestled in a narrow feeder canyon southeast of the main one, he veered from the killers' path entirely.

Ten minutes later, he hunkered down inside an aban-doned harness shop, which was not much more than a ten-by-ten-foot log box with nary a furnishing remaining inside and all its windows wide open to the weather, its rear and front doors missing. He crunched through the snow lying in ripples and small drifts upon the packed earthen floor, pressed a shoulder to the building's front wall, and edged a careful look through the shutterless window left of the gaping front door.

From here he could see the two sets of tracks moving into the old, abandoned village from the left. They an-gled toward the stone shack hunched amongst firs and cedars almost directly across the street.

The hovel, which had a shake-shingled roof, was nearly concealed by trees that had grown up around it since it had been abandoned. But Longarm could still see a thin tendril of wood smoke rising from the dented tin chim-ney pipe and curling against the dark green fir boughs. A shingle above the closed Z-frame timber door announced in badly faded letters CONSTABLE. A window on each side of the door was shuttered.

Looking up and down the short, snowy street on which a dozen or so buildings sat facing each other, Longarm saw that the constable's office was the best preserved. And it had a functioning wood stove.

The obvious choice for a passel of killers to hide out in.

He ran a gloved hand across his mustache and considered his options. There weren't many. Judging from the tracks and the smoke, the killers were holed up in the old hoosegow this very moment. They had the door and shutters closed, so they couldn't see him unless the cracks between the boards of the shutters and door timbers were wide enough.

He grunted and spat as he walked over to the harness shop's doorless front opening. He held his pistol straight down by his side and thumbed the hammer back with a ratcheting click. Stepping outside, he glanced quickly up and down the street, then tramped straight out away from the harness shop. His heart beating insistently, his eyes glued to the door of the jailhouse, he crossed the snow-drifted street in seconds.

He grabbed the Z-frame door's iron handle, and pulled.

He was surprised at how easily the door came open. It banged against the building's front wall as he stepped inside, then put his back to the wall right of the door, so the gaping doorway wouldn't backlight him, and extended his pistol straight out from his shoulder.

He held fire as he looked around the room, squinting into the dense brown shadows. His nostrils were assailed by the thick fetor of unwashed bodies and rotten food. Nothing moved. The hovel, which was only slightly larger than the harness shop he'd just left, was cluttered with tin plates and cups and gnawed bones of small animals as well as large ones—deer, maybe a small bear. Most of this was spread across a single table shoved against the front wall to Longarm's left, but there was more on the floor amongst tack and blankets. On the floor in front of one of the three jail cells lined up against the back wall, was a pyramid of unopened vegetable tins—tomatoes, beans, and spinach.

Amidst the food mess and dirty plates on the table was an old-model Colt pistol and several empty ammo boxes and a cartridge belt with only one of its leather loops showing the brass of a live round. A large, blood-crusted skinning knife poked up out of the table, gray light pushing through cracks in the shutter in front of it, bathing the hide-wrapped handle.

On the stove in front of Longarm, around which several crude pallets and blankets and furs had been arranged, a battered black coffeepot chugged and wheezed. The small fire in the stove snapped dully. Longarm could see the orange glow around the dented steel door.

He moved forward, swinging his cocked Colt around before him. In the dimness, he saw something on the floor in the cell farthest left. Heading toward it slowly, he almost kicked an overfilled slop bucket, the heavy latrine stench of which nearly made him gag. Wincing against it, he continued on into the cell and looked down at the long figure—obviously a body—over which bobcat hides had been tossed.

With a cautious glance toward the open door behind him, which was a rectangle of dull gray light stitched with grainy snowflakes, he peeled the robes down to reveal the hollow-cheeked, patch-bearded face of the dead man. Longarm hadn't seen his assailant clearly in last night's darkness and blowing snow, but this was likely him. When he pulled the robes down still farther and saw the bloody mess he'd made of the man's belly with three .44-40 rounds drilled from point-blank range, he was sure.

Longarm took a close look at the man. Maybe mid-twenties, but old for his years. His eyes were gray-blue and widely staring with a mania that remained even in death, and his hair was hacked off short above his ears. Nothing distinctive about him, except his clothes were smoke- and food-stained, badly wash-worn. Except his boots. They'd been hand sewn from several prime jack-rabbit hides, and a skinning knife jutted up from the right one, its bone handle just visible above the shaggy fur.

The hands at his sides were thick, hard-calloused, and badly scarred, with a couple fingertips missing, and they seemed to belong to a man twice this man's age, some-one who'd lived an incredibly hard life in rough country. Likely, mountain country.

Longarm tossed the hides back over the killer's head. As he started to push up from his knees, something sounded outside the cabin's door.

There was a faint boot crunch and then a wood scrape.

The lawman jerked himself straight and swung his .44 toward the open doorway, squinting an eye as he aimed down the barrel. "Show yourself, you son of a bitch!"

Chapter 16

An eye and part of a black cap poked out from behind the doorjamb, on the door's right side and about four feet up from the floor. The eye brightened, and the mouth twisted a shit-eating grin.

Longarm tipped his pistol barrel up and depressed the hammer. "Clancy!"

The boy stepped into the doorway, grinning like his bull had just received a prize at the county fair. "Was you gonna shoot me?"

"What the hell're you doin' out here, son?" Longarm crossed the room in three long strides and hauled the boy into the jailhouse by one little arm clad in shabby green wool and, crouching, looked around outside where the snow was falling harder, though so far the wind hadn't picked up. He noted two sets of rumpled tracks leading away from the doorway and around the hovel's far side.

"I seen you come this way."

"What were you doin' outside, boy?"

"Hell if I know."

Longarm stood in the doorway, looking around for

signs of the killers—at least two more on the loose. And now Longarm had the boy to worry about.

"You shouldn't be out here, son."

"I thought you done kilt the howlin' maniac."

"I did, but—"

"Did you see them spooks?"

Longarm whipped around, frowning down at the little lad looking lumpy in his wool coat and trousers and rubber overshoes, a black wool cap pulled down low on his forehead. Two red dots big as silver dollars rode high on his pale cheeks, and green snot oozed from his nose; he kept sniffing at it, but it remained there above his red upper lip.

"Spooks?"

The little boy hooked a mittened thumb to his right, canting his head. "Them two makin' off through the trees yonder. They didn't see me. I hunkered down low, in case they was Injuns. At first I thought they were bears or such, but then I seen they were just fellas dressed in furs."

"Where'd you see 'em, Clancy?"

The little boy stepped to the door and looked up the narrow street of the old part of Sully Creek, in the direction of the Trinity. "Back that way."

"Headin' toward the hotel?"

"That's right." The boy threw his head back on his shoulders to stare up at the tall lawman looming over him. His eyes sparked eagerly, and he sniffed at the green goober once more in futility. "Who are they? You gonna have to kill them bastards, too?"

Longarm stepped into the street, looking up the snowy canyon toward the main village.

He could see a couple of humble shacks on the north

ridge wall, above nearer pines, but not much else. There were more pines to the right, at the base of a low, rocky ridge. The killers must have deposited their partner here, then stole off around the back of the jailhouse, keeping to the cover of the pines at the ridge's base.

They were out there now, heading toward the village and, doubtless, more killing.

Longarm moved back to the boy watching him with eager expectance from the jailhouse doorway. "How'd you get out here, you little rawhider, you? You must have nearly drowned in them drifts."

"I bulled right through that snow. Nobody's tougher'n me. Back home I helped my pa cut wood and such, though we won't be doin' that no more as we're headin' for Utah and Pa's gonna open his own store with Grandpa, though Momma don't like it on account o' she thinks Grandpa's a skinflint."

Longarm holstered his six-shooter, gave his back to the boy, and crouched down. "Just the same, climb up here on my back."

The boy did as he was told, lacing his hands around Longarm's neck and jumping up onto his back, piggy-back style. "What for?"

"'Cause we're gonna get you back to the Trinity pronto."

"What for?"

"'Cause there's gonna be more trouble, I think." Longarm started back through the snow, angling across the street on an intersection course with his own tracks from the hotel/saloon. With the boy on his back, he needed plenty of cover, and that route offered the best cover out here.

"You really think so?" The boy didn't sound disappointed.

"Hush, now, Clancy. Make like we're army soldiers or such, and we're on the trail of Apaches. You know how good Apaches can hear, right?"

In the corner of his eye, the boy nodded his head.

"All right, then . . ."

Longarm high-stepped through the deep drifts, angling around old corrals, tripping around sundry objects the snow had buried, and dropped down into the ravine, the snow rising up around his hips in places. At the bottom, he took a deep breath and hoofed it up the other side, his heart hammering from the extra weight and the steep climb on slippery terrain.

Something large and black appeared from behind a snow-laden fir. The thing howled and squawked loudly, making Longarm's eardrums ache. There was a great rushing sound.

Blood jetting in his veins, Longarm released Clancy's legs and reached for the grips of the Colt jutting above his coat. At the same time, his boot slipped out from under him, and he and the boy fell back and sideways, Longarm landing in the deep snow on his left shoulder and feeling one of the boy's knees beneath him.

Both he and the boy grunted loudly.

Longarm's ears rang from the horrible din before him, and certain that a knife slash or a bullet was imminent, he clawed his Colt out of its holster and, thumbing back the hammer, extended the snowy piece out and up in front of him. He stayed his trigger finger, eyes widening in shock to see a large, black raven sort of hovering and cawing hysterically in the air in front of him and Clancy.

The bird gave another cry, flapping its large wings with the sound of a rug beaten with a broom, then managed to swing itself around and fly up, around the snow-laden fir, and out of sight.

"Shit!" Clancy intoned. "I thought our goose was coo—!"

He cut himself off when Longarm twisted around, pressing a finger to his lips.

As the raven's cries died gradually in the gray, snowy distance, Longarm stooped low so the boy could climb up on his back again, and they set off once more, weaving around trees and boulders and dilapidated chicken coops. As they crossed another, shallow ravine, the rears of several buildings at the town's east edge shoved up on their right, and Longarm kept his eyes on them, cautious of the killers' movements.

They likely knew he was out here and, what's more, they probably knew he'd killed their friend. They'd been kill crazy before, but now he had to assume that they'd be even more blood hungry.

He was glad to see the rear of the Trinity with the big pile of cordwood stacked against its rear, under an outside stairs zigzagging down from the upper stories and fairly sagging beneath its heavy snow burden.

"Clancy!" the boy's mother fairly screamed when she saw the boy riding Longarm piggyback through the door flanking the bar. The pregnant, obviously distraught woman turned from a group of men—one of the saddle tramps, Scotty, and the boy's father—who'd been gathered near the front door, pulling on coats and hats, the saddle tramp checking the loads in his old Schofield revolver.

She came running and, when Longarm had dropped the boy from his back, swept him up in his arms. "Where've you been? I've been so worried about you, Clancy!"

"Just out grubbin' around, Ma."

"I told you to stay near the hotel."

"But, but, but . . ." Clancy cast Longarm a desperate look. "The marshal said it was okay."

"Oh, he did, did he?"

Longarm gave a wry chuff and left the woman cajoling the boy back near the bar and headed toward the front of the room. The father tramped on past him, looking harried and disgusted as he unbuttoned his long fur coat. Bill Carson was shoving more wood into the potbellied stove, and as Longarm tramped to a front window, the hotel proprietor said, "You find the dead maniac?"

"I found him."

"Where?" Scotty wanted to know, his clean forehead deeply lined.

"Back in the old part of town. Found their den. Livin' like the three fuckin' bears. Two were headed this way, and I 'spect they maybe took exception to how I treated their kith or kin or whoever the crazy bastard was."

"Well, maybe we oughta just go out and introduce ourselves." The saddle tramp held up his pistol. His mackinaw was unbuttoned, and his eyes were red, his face pasty behind his beard. "Let 'em shake hands with Mr. Schofield here."

Longarm looked at him like he was something someone dragged in on muddy boots. "Where's your friend?"

"With one of the whores."

Looking around, Longarm saw both Hollis and Rappaporte eating bacon and eggs at a nearby table with the dark, lanky Parson Fitzgerald, all three regarding Longarm with curious expectance. "The other girls alone?" he directed a scowl at Hollis.

"Sylvus Nordstrom's with Wilomena," Rappaporte said, forking bacon into his mouth. "That big bastard just can't get enough o' that pricey lovin'. What I want to know, Marshal, is what you intend to do about those other two killers running off their leashes out yonder? While you and the younker were out throwing snowballs, they could have been in here, feeding their bloodlust!"

Longarm turned to Scotty. "We gotta herd everyone in town into the hotel. I don't want anyone out yonder alone—especially the women. The hermit likely won't come, and he can probably protect himself just fine, but we'd best tell 'im how it is and leave the decision to him."

Scotty pursed his lips. "Want me to go over and talk to him?"

Longarm nodded, then turned to the saddle tramp. "Holster that hogleg, Mr. Schofield. I'm gonna fetch my rifle and then you and me are gonna go over and fetch the girls and their customers."

The saddle tramp said, "The name's Roy, and me and the Schofield are ready to put an end to this bullshit."

As Longarm headed for the stairs at the back of the room, the conductor, Hollis, called, "Custis, you got any idea who they are yet? Them crazy killers?"

Longarm turned to the man. His own befuddlement must have shone on his face, because Scotty said from up near the front door, "You had it right, Marshal. They're the three bears. Or were. Just like rogue grizzlies. Some men get that way up here in these mountains, after so long alone. They go wild and rogue and start goin' through villages the way a grizzly'll go through a herd of cattle or the way wolves or coyotes'll lay waste to a flock of sheep. There ain't no explainin' it. And the only way to stop 'em is to hunt 'em down and shoot 'em."

With that, Scotty snugged a thick wool hat down tight on his bullet-shaped head, hefted a rifle in his gloved hands, and went out.

Roy stared at the closed door, then turned to Longarm and gave a caustic, disbelieving chuff. "The three bears? Bullshit."

Longarm tramped up the narrow stairs climbing the rear wall over the bar. From the second story, he could hear the wind picking up outside, making the timbers groan. He could also hear a raspy, mannish voice from behind Janice Hathaway's door. He knocked twice before pushing the door open.

"Custis!" Janice said, casting him a relieved smile again as she sat in her wrapper and fur coat at the edge of her bed, nervously grinding one delicate bare foot atop the other.

Flora sat in front of the window on the other side of the room from Longarm, her high-topped, lace-up boots crossed on the scarred wooden table as she lounged in a spool-back chair that she'd tipped back on its rear legs. Flora's man's hat was on the table, and she was smoking a quirley, her long, greasy hair hanging past her shoulders. She gave Longarm a piqued look as Janice suddenly frowned and said, "Flora here tells me the killer's still on the loose. She suggests I don't look out the window into the street but refused to tell me why."

"Flora's right," Longarm said. "Best stay away from the window for a time, Janice."

"My men," the actress said with a cautious, knowing air. "They're . . . out there, aren't they?"

Flora blew a thin smoke plume at the ceiling above the bed. "Now, don't you worry your pretty little head, Miss Hathaway. Soon, this storm'll be over and this tall, dark drink o' water here's gonna find out what in a jasper's June is goin' on around here. He'll have them killers skewered over hot fires, and you'll be headin' out on the old narrow gauge."

Janice made a face and turned back to Longarm, who picked up his rifle and jacked a round into the chamber. "Killers?"

Longarm glanced reprovingly at Flora, who scowled and turned away, sheepish. "There's two more," he said. "Only there's about to be no more. I'm goin' out after 'em just as soon as I get everyone in village—especially the girls—safe inside the saloon here. You just stay up here with Flora. You'll be safe here."

Longarm turned to the door.

"Custis!"

Janice rushed toward him and threw her arms around his neck, pressing her heaving bosom up tight against his chest. "I'm scared." She glanced at Flora, a touch of revulsion in her gaze. "I mean, I feel safe here with Flora and all, but . . . I'm worried about you. And what if you can't get these killers?"

"Ah, the lawdog'll get him," Flora said, knocking ashes off her quirley, then, pinching it between thumb and index finger and lifting it to her lips, added, "They're likely just a couple of addled mountain men runnin' off their nuts. They'll slip up, and Lawdog'll grease 'em. And shit, if he don't—hell, I will!"

Flora threw head back and laughed her raspy, raucous laugh.

Longarm placed a hand on Janice's back, drew her to him, and kissed her tenderly. He gave her a wink, peeled himself from the girl's frightened embrace, headed into the hall, and drew the door closed behind him.

Chapter 17

Longarm tied his scarf over his hat, donned gloves, scooped his rifle off the table, and turned to Roy standing near the door, his own rifle on his shoulder. "Ready?"

Roy, looking grimly determined, spit chaw into a nearby sandbox. "Let's get this done."

Longarm reached for the door handle but stopped when Hollis, standing with several others in a semicircle around him and Roy, said, "You want me and Rappaporte to go out there with you, Custis?" He formed an expression that was half smile, half wince and turned his head a little to one side in dread.

Rappaporte scowled at the conductor and, thumbing his spats, said to Longarm sheepishly, "Unfortunately, I've . . . I've never been very handy with a gun."

The others behind and around him—the drummers and the miners and Fitzgerald—looked around and down and suddenly got busy toeing the floorboards.

Longarm said, "The more men we have out there, the more likely we'll be to shoot each other. You all stay here, make sure the doors remain locked. Answer any knocks only after you've looked out the window to see who it is. Scotty oughta be back soon with or without the hermit. Tell him to stay put. Me and Roy should be back in a couple minutes with the girls."

Noting a collective, silent sigh of relief amongst the small group before him, he opened the door, looked around, and went out. The snow was coming down nearly as hard as it had yesterday, and the wind was starting to moan and mewl like rabid warlocks. When Roy had stepped out behind him, closing the door, Longarm pulled his hat brim low and started quickly down the porch steps. "Stay close. It's getting damn bad out here!"

Longarm jogged across the snowy street, glancing up at Janice's four dead thugs, who twisted and turned on their ropes in the howling wind, and tramped across the bridge. Roy stayed within a few feet of his heels, and together they jogged along the main street's north side, heading west past cabins and two- or three-story business buildings with their shingle chains jangling loudly. On their left, the creek's cold, black water churned along its twisting, snowy bed, furry wedges of gray ice creeping out from both banks.

Approaching Miss Tulip's cabin, Longarm turned to Roy. "I'll fetch Miss Tulip and your partner." He canted his head toward the cabin on the rocky rise flanking the sporting girl's shack. "You go on up and tell Miss Wilomena and her jake to get dressed, and wait for 'em. Don't leave 'em alone. I'll be up in a minute to fetch Miss Rae."

Roy jogged off around Miss Tulip's cabin, heading toward the snow-buried steps rising toward Miss Wilomena's gray shack. Longarm, noting lantern light in Miss

Tulip's frosted windows, knocked on the door. Hearing no movement inside, he rapped again and called, "Miss Tulip?"

Nothing but the wind and the snow ticking off the shack's stout front wall.

Longarm raised his Winchester, cocking the hammer and stepping a few feet back from the door. He was about to raise his right foot to kick the door in when there was the rasp of locking bar being lifted from iron brackets. The door latch clicked, and a girl's blue eye squinted out the crack between the door and the frame.

"Miss Tulip?"

The girl pulled the door open. "Just bein' careful," she said. "I heard you'd done caught the—"

Longarm pushed inside, and the girl, dressed in a black velvet robe trimmed in red and holding a wine-glass in one hand, a long black cheroot in the other, stepped back, frowning. "What's goin' on, Longarm?"

He looked around the cabin. The woodstove chugged, pushing heat against him. There wasn't much to the place, so it was easy to see that Miss Tulip was alone.

Longarm heaved the door closed against the wind. "Where's the saddle tramp?"

"What saddle tramp?"

"Roy's friend."

Miss Tulip scrunched her face up with incredulity. "Who's Roy?"

"You're alone out here?"

"Well, shit, I been hopin' for more customers since ole Rapp left, but I figured everyone in the village was afraid of their damn shadow. I was fixin' to come on over to the hotel and hustle up some business my own self, but"—she smiled, rheumy-eyed from drink, and started to raise an arm toward Longarm's neck—"now that you're here."

"Get dressed," Longarm said, dodging the girl's embrace to look out the window right of the door. "The hotel's the safest place for you. There's two more killers on the prowl." He peered both directions up the street, wondering if Roy's partner had chosen one of the other two whores instead of Tulip, or if he was lost out there somewhere or dead and about to be trussed up like Janice's thugs.

"Ah, hell!" Tulip planted a fist on her hip. "You sure about that?"

Longarm turned to the girl, placed a hand on her cheek. "Now, would I lie to you, Miss Tulip? In case you hadn't looked out your window lately, there's four men—big, powerful men—hanging from that cotton-wood over by the Trinity."

"No shit?" She brushed past him to look out the window. "Is that what them things are?"

"That's what they are." He took the drink out of her hand and set in on a table. "Now, shake a leg, Miss Tulip. Get yourself bundled up. I'm gonna go up and fetch Miss Rae, and while I'm gone, I want you to keep the door locked and don't let anyone in but me. Understand?"

The gravity of the situation seemed to penetrate the girl's inebriation; she nodded, set her cheroot on the edge of the table, then followed Longarm to the door. He heard her dropping the locking bar into place as he grimaced against the wind poking its cold hand down under his raised coat collar and jogged around the shack's far side.

Miss Rae's shack was farther back from Miss Tulip's than Miss Wilomena's, and it was fronted by two gnarled cedars bent low under the thrashing wind. He made it up the snow-buried steps with effort and, breathing hard, pounded the girl's door as he shouted, "It's Deputy U.S. Marshal Custis Long, Miss Rae! I'd like to take you over to the hotel for a spell!"

No answer.

"Christ," he muttered and rapped again. "Miss Rae?"

Again, only the wind and the snow answered him.

He shuffled left to peek into a window, but the glass was coated in a good quarter inch of solid ice. He moved back to the door, knocked again, and froze with his hand in mid-knock as the door that apparently hadn't been closed tight squawked open a few inches. He lowered his hand to his rifle, wrapping it around the rifle's forestock, and scowling through the crack between the door and the frame, said, "Miss Rae?"

He waited five seconds, then stepped back and slammed his right boot against the door, sending it flying wide as he bolted forward to catch the door against his right shoulder as it bounced off the wall and aimed the Winchester straight out from his right shoulder.

"Ah, hell," he raked out, scrunching his weathered handsome features into a mask of dread and revulsion.

Miss Rae's cabin was no larger than Miss Tulip's, so it wasn't hard to see that the girl was alone. And it wasn't hard to see that she was dead, sprawled naked on her back across the four-by-four-foot eating table in the cabin's center, under a glowing bull's-eye lantern that cast a buttery glow across her black-skinned body that was covered—all that Longarm could see of it from the door, and he didn't care to inspect it very closely just now—in what appeared a good gallon of fresh blood. His shocked, horrified gaze had just found the grisly gashes over her chest and belly when he was aware of someone in the doorway behind him.

He whipped around, heart fluttering, aiming the Winchester straight out in front of him with both hands. He slackened his trigger finger when he saw Roy staring at him from just outside the open doorway. The saddle tramp's face was flour-white behind his beard, and his eyes were stricken, dazed. Dancing snowflakes caught in his beard that was damp with what appeared to be vomit.

Roy canted his head slightly, to look into the cabin beyond Longarm then, drawing his lips wide in a grimace, he swallowed, ran a wrist across his mouth, and said, "The other whore and the drummer . . ."

"What?" Longarm urged, his own brain still reeling from his own grisly findings.

"They're dead, too. Out back o' the cabin. Butchered."

Longarm lowered the rifle.

"You seen Bob?" Roy asked him in a voice the lawman could barely hear above the yammering, intensifying storm.

Longarm shook his head. "He didn't make it over here."

Roy's nostrils flared. "They got him, too." He turned and staggered a few feet beyond the cabin, and as Longarm stepped out and pulled the door closed behind, Roy bellowed, "I'm gonna kill you fuckin' savage bastards!" He raised his rifle and triggered three quick shots skyward, smoke and flames stabbing from the barrel, the old Spencer belching like firecrackers against the wind.

Longarm lunged toward the man, gritting his teeth with rage, but before he could grab Roy's rifle, he heard a whisper in his left ear and felt a stitch in the wind in front of his face. There was a solid plunking sound. Roy grunted and snapped his head to the right, away from Longarm, and dropped his rifle. Longarm stared in renewed shock at the man's whose head straightened on his shoulders and sort of wobbled around as though his neck had been snapped. Then, as Roy dropped to his knees, Longarm saw the ragged hole in his hat crown and saw the red staining the snow beyond him. As he realized the man had been shot, it occurred to him that one of the rifle reports he'd heard had not belonged to Roy's Spencer but to some other gun off to Longarm's left.

Roy fell facedown in the snow, and Longarm wheeled to his left, bringing up his Winchester. He could see nothing but a few scrub pines, boulders, and Miss Wilomena's cabin through the billowing curtains of wind-driven snow. A scream sounded—high and horrified—and he looked down the long slope in front of him to see a fur-clad figure standing at the rear of Miss Tulip's cabin, facing Longarm, long hair blowing in the wind. At first, he thought it was one of the killers, then he recognized Miss Tulip's slender figure inside the buffalo robe, saw the hands raised to her face.

He bolted forward and down the slope so quickly that he lost his footing on the snow-covered steps. He hit the ground, rolled, somehow managing to hold on to his Winchester, and gained his feet at the bottom of the incline. Expecting another shot from the hidden sniper at any moment, he heaved himself to his feet, grabbed the girl's hand, and began pulling her around her cabin.

"Come on!"

Miss Tulip groaned and sobbed as he half dragged her out into the main street and then across the snowy bridge, looking around wildly for the killers, whom he could sense stalking him, whom he imagined in every wind and snow blast, whom he saw or imagined he saw darting back behind awning posts or ducking under hitch racks, planting a bead on him or the girl or maybe both at the same time.

As he gained the other side of the bridge, the girl dropped to her knees in a snowdrift. "Goddamnit, I can't walk that fast!"

Longarm cursed, shifted his rifle to one hand, and picked the girl up in his arms. He carried her up the Trinity's porch steps, and kicked the door twice with his right boot, yelling his name. Voices rose behind the door, and boots hammered the puncheons. He kicked again, and when he was about to kick a fourth time, the door opened, and an owl-eyed Bill Carson stepped back as Longarm stumbled inside and set Miss Tulip down on her feet.

Shivering and hunched forward, arms crossed on her chest, Tulip looked up anxiously at the lawman. "That other fella—was he . . . ?"

"Dead."

Carson scowled. "Who's dead now?"

"Roy." Longarm glanced at Parson Fitzgerald, who looked almost sober. "Get her over to the fire, will you, Parson? Fetch her somethin' hot to drink."

As the parson did as he'd been instructed, Miss Tulip glanced back at Longarm. "What about Wilomena?" Her eyes were anguished. "Miss Rae?"

Longarm closed the door and walked over to the window on its right, peering into the storm, his brows hooded with consternation. Damn this weather. Those killers were going to be mighty hard to track in the cold and the blowing snow.

Carson stepped up beside Longarm. "Yeah, what about the others you was fetchin'?"

Longarm continued staring outside as he said through his teeth. "Dead. Butchered. They shot Roy. As for his partner, I reckon he's dead, too."

"You get a look at 'em?"

Longarm turned to see Scotty flanking him beside the short, bandy-legged hotel owner. He was still wearing his hat, which was dappled with melted snow, and his coat was unbuttoned. In his ham-sized fist, he held a steaming cup of coffee.

"Nah," Longarm growled. "They're like ghosts. What about the hermit?"

"He wasn't there."

"Not there?"

"The cabin was cold and dark."

Longarm just stared at the man, who stared back at him darkly. The lawman didn't know what to think about that. Was the hermit one of the killers?

He stepped back away from the window and told the others to do likewise. "At least one of 'em has a rifle," he said. "And he ain't afraid to use it."

As the others shuffled anxiously away from the window, cursing and murmuring amongst themselves, the

parson sitting with the sobbing Miss Tulip near the crackling stove, Scotty continued boring holes through Longarm with his hard, dark eyes. "The weather's in their
favor, ain't it? They know where we are, but we don't
know where in the hell they are. Hell, they're liable to
start shootin' through the windows, take out as many of us
as they can. We wouldn't have nothin' to shoot back at."

Pressing his back between the door and the window,
Longarm kept his voice low. "I reckon that's about the
size of it. You still game, Scotty?"

"For what?"

"For goin' out there and stalkin' those ringtails? Blowin'
'em into the next fuckin' universe."

The big, bald man didn't look as eager as he had
been before, but he nodded just the same. "I'll back your
play, lawman. How we gonna keep from shootin' each
other?"

"We'll each take an end of town and start workin' our
way back toward the Trinity." To the rest of the room,
Longarm said, "The rest of you stay put. No one goes
outside." He frowned to see Janice Hathaway hauling a
pot of coffee in from the saloon's back room. Her eyes
met his. "I couldn't just sit up there like the queen of
Egypt," she said, fear making her voice husky. "I decided to come down here and help out Mr. Carson."

"She don't look like she would be, but she ain't half-
bad kitchen help," Carson quipped, trying in vain to
lighten the mood.

As Janice poured a cup of coffee into a stone mug
and gave the mug to Miss Tulip, Longarm turned to
Scotty. "Ready?"

"Ready as I'll ever be."

Longarm turned to open the front door.

In the second story, a shrill scream sounded. Shrill and raspy, it turned to an exasperated sob that dwindled gradually.

"Ah, ya bloody bastard!" Flora cried. Then, louder, causing everyone in the room to jerk their frightened eyes toward the stairs down which the mannish woman came slowly, on wobbly legs and holding her hands over her belly: *"Ah, ya bloody bastard—what'd ya have to go an' kill me for?"*

Chapter 18

Longarm pushed through the small crowd gathered in front of him and ran to the back of the saloon, kicking chairs out of his way. He climbed the stairs two steps at a time, until he was standing over Flora, who'd slumped down against the brick wall, blood and viscera oozing through the hole in her middle and spilling down her man's soiled, patched duck trousers.

She was grimacing, sobbing, and shivering as the life left her.

"Ah, shit!" Longarm snarled, genuinely grieved for the woman.

Upstairs, a shrill scream sounded, jerking his attention toward the second story. He turned toward Scotty and Janice, who were rushing up the stairs behind him, heading toward the fast-dying Flora. "Tend her!"

He bolted on up the stairs, taking three steps at a time now and holding his Winchester in his right hand, pulling himself up the steps with the other rail. Rounding the corner at the top of the stairs and heading down the dingy hall, he thought, What in Christ am I gonna find now?

The commotion was happening toward the hall's far end, but he couldn't see the brunt of it until he'd bulled past Clancy's father, who was pulling the boy's obviously horrified, sobbing mother back into their room. Clancy himself stood near the open door, back pressed against the hall's wall, staring toward the end of the hall, where the stout German woman seemed to be engaged in some sort of foofaraw with a bear—or at least a big man in a bear coat.

"No, Mother, no!" the woman's husband cajoled, trying to get his hands on the fireplace poker with which she was pummeling the snarling beast's long-haired head.

The woman was bellowing in German, sort of slipping and sliding in a slick blood pool on the floor. To her left, the outside door, accessed by the rear outside stairs, stood half open, and snow blew through the crack. The big man—Longarm could see that the intruder was indeed a man clad in a long, bear-hide greatcoat and wearing a thick, bib-length salt-and-pepper beard—was slipping and sliding in the blood, as well, and that was the reason he hadn't yet gutted the old German woman with the enormous, bloody knife in his hand.

The knife he'd apparently gutted Miss Flora with.

His face was red behind his beard, and his dark eyes were huge with fury. His long silver-streaked hair—the top of his head was completely bald—danced about his coat's wide collar, and he bellowed like a poleaxed bull as he slashed with the knife while parrying the German lady's savage blows with his other arm.

"Go with your ma and pa, Clancy!" Longarm yelled at the gaping boy as he ran past him, raising his Winchester to get a shot at the interloper, whose fetor filled the lawman's nose like especially strong vinegar.

"Get out of the way, fräulein!" he ordered the tireless German woman.

But just as he got himself stopped in the middle of the hall and had levered and raised his Winchester, the man-beast gave a yowl as, trying to duck away from the woman's blows and having one of his fur boots slip out from beneath him, he plunged straight back through the window behind him. There was a crash of breaking glass and wooden sashes beneath the woman's loud German curses, and the man was gone, replaced by tassels of snow blowing in through the ragged opening.

"There—take that you smelly wolf!" the old woman yelled, stooped over the window to stare down at her handiwork.

Longarm cursed and ran on down the hall, slipping and nearly falling in the blood near the end, and shoved the stocky German woman away from the drafty window. "Out of the way, damnit!"

"Don't push me!" She raised the poker as if to lay into Longarm with it, her eyes wide with fury and spittle flying from her lips.

"Momma, come!" her one-eyed old husband, clad in a striped sleeping gown and nightcap cajoled her, grabbing both her thick arms and managing to drag her back to the open door of their room.

With his Winchester's barrel, Longarm held the fluttering drapes away from the broken window and stared down into the gap between the Trinity and the next building, just able to make out a gray figure thrashing in the deeply drifted snow directly below him.

The lawman didn't bother with the usual warnings and pleas for surrender; these man-beasts didn't deserve it. Quickly raising the rifle to his shoulder, he aimed into the gap. A particularly heavy wind gust nudged the rifle barrel sideways, and he had to reset his feet before triggering five fast rounds into the heavy, howling whiteout, peppering the gap directly below the window.

When the snow cleared, he saw the gray figure bolting to his left and around the rear corner of the building on the other side of the gap.

"Shit!" Longarm shouted into the wind.

How could he have missed the son of a bitch?

Impulsively, he leaped up onto the window ledge, then, holding his rifle tightly in his right hand, heaved himself out the window and into the icy wind and pelting snow. His breath was sucked from his lungs with a ragged wheeze. His stomach leaped into his throat. His boots plunged into the deep, downy drift, and he suddenly found himself half sitting, half lying, and almost entirely buried in the frigid drift, icy snow tentacles reaching under his collar and slithering down the front of his coat.

He thrashed around until he got himself to his feet and then thrashed some more until he'd gained the corner of the building beyond the Trinity, where the snow was shallower. He bolted around the corner and set off running as fast as the snow would allow, following the tracks of the murderous maniac that were clearly etched in front of him though already filling with snakelike fingers of wind-driven snow.

The cold gnawed at his ears and blew his hair about his head. Having removed his scarf in the saloon, he must have lost his hat in his plunge from the window.

He followed the tracks into an alley between two buildings. Ahead in the inky grayness, a gun flashed. The bullet plunked into a half-buried pile of lumber to his right. The wind lightened momentarily, and he saw the big man-beast standing crouched at the alley mouth, extending a revolver.

Longarm threw himself left as the gun flashed again. The bullet sizzled through the howling wind.

Longarm heaved himself to a knee, raising the Winchester that was caked with snow, and as he got his finger on the trigger he saw that the man had vanished into the swirling storm fog. He pushed to his feet and trudged deliberately through the knee-deep powder, heading toward the mouth of the gap while aiming the Winchester out from his right side, ready to shoot at the first sign of movement.

He gained the corner of the undertaker's shed and surveyed the street in front of him. He couldn't see much but the blowing snow and the vague outlines of cabins on the other side of the creek-cleaved street. Stepping out around the shed, he saw a man-shaped figure before him and swung the rifle hard left.

Instantly, the man raised his arms high above his head, one hand wrapped around the stock of an old Springfield Trapdoor, and bellowed, "It's Engel! Don't shoot me, damnit!"

An amalgam of relief and anger washed over Longarm's jittery nerves. "Goddamnit, Engel!"

"He headed thataway!" The man turned to point west. "Toward the train station!"

Longarm bolted forward. Engel grabbed his arm, and

Longarm glanced back at the undertaker, who was wrapped in a thick blanket coat and mufflers through which a snowy beard and watery hazel eyes shone. "You want some help?"

"Go back inside and stay there till I tell ya it's safe!" Longarm shouted above the wind.

"I was hopin' you'd say that!"

As Engel bolted toward his cracked shed door, Longarm ran past him, spying the recent tracks in the drifting snow that ran close to the street's left side, often crossing boardwalks and showing that the killer lengthened his stride as he passed gaps between shops and cabins. The long, low depot building, flanked by the stalled train, had just started to take shape in front of him when he stopped suddenly. A figure darted out from a springhouse fronting the depot, on the building's left and nearly straight ahead of Longarm, who was standing atop the small stone constable office's rickety covered stoop.

Longarm's pulse kicked up a throbbing in his temple. He bolted forward off the stoop and stopped in a wind-cleared patch of frozen street, raising his Winchester. When the killer's bulky, dark brown figure was halfway between the springhouse and the depot, Longarm planted a bead on the man's back, just below his neck, and squeezed the trigger. The Winchester leaped and roared a half second after the man had stumbled over something buried in the snow and dropped to a knee.

Longarm's bullet careened over the man's head to plunk soundlessly into the front of the depot building.

"Shit!" The wind instantly tore and shredded the lawman's wail.

The killer jerked his head around toward Longarm, who quickly racked another cartridge into the Winchester's breech. The man jerked several times, obviously having trouble gaining his feet, and a subtle thrill swept like a fleeting but balmy zephyr through the federal badge toter's chest.

He must have hit the beast when he'd fired from the Trinity's second story.

As the killer gained his feet with a desperate heave, flapping his arms like wings, Longarm fired two more shots. If the slugs hit their target, Longarm couldn't tell, for the killer high-stepped unflinchingly through the deep snow and into the dense shadows beneath the depot's overhanging roof.

Longarm glimpsed the door opening and closing, a blur of gray movement, and he loosed another frustrated curse as he ran forward, dropped to a knee, and emptied the Winchester, hearing a couple of his slugs plunking into the door and shattering windows before the hammer pinged benignly against the firing pin.

He regained his feet and, reaching under his coat, plucked fresh shells from his cartridge belt and fed them through the Winchester's loading gate.

He was breathing hard, staring through narrowed eyes at the depot obscured by wavering snow curtains.

When he'd shoved four shells into the rifle, he took off running toward the stationhouse, feeding five more through the loading gate before gaining the covered area outside the front door. He'd just begun to wonder if the killer had snuck out the trackside door when a blurry gray figure moved behind one of the two large, rectan-

gular windows right of the door, and he threw himself
behind an awning post.

A gun flashed on the other side of the window and a
ping of breaking glass was accompanied by the pop of a
six-shooter. There were two more shots, both plunking
into the awning post, making the post shudder against
Longarm's back and shoulders. The lawman bolted out
from behind the post and drilled two rounds through the
window before sidestepping out of the path of an ex-
pected return shot.

He spread his boots and quickly, calmly hammered
two more slugs through the broken window before charging to the front door. His blood was boiling, rage swell-
ing like miniature hearts in his temples. The door flew
open easily under his right boot heel, and he blew through
the opening as the door slammed against the wall. He
fired and levered, fired and levered, filling the close confines with the rifle's echoing roars, and clouding the shadowy air in front of him with billowing powder smoke.

He'd concentrated his shooting on the trackside door,
before which the killer's bulky shadow had been moving. Now the figure simply leaned back against the door
that the man had been trying to open, convulsing and
snarling like a wounded, rabid dog. Longarm stood holding his empty, still-smoking Winchester in front of him
while the man made a choking sound and slowly slid
down the door to the floor, extending his legs straight out
in front of him. There was the clack of a pistol hitting
the floor between his legs.

Longarm looked around the empty, smoky room.

Where was the other kill-crazy son of a bitch?

He looked around cautiously once more, reaching under his coat for a cartridge, but instead of plucking the cartridge from his shell belt, he stooped over the convulsing man before him and used his rifle butt to shove the man's head back against the door. He stared into the man's eyes. The killer's long beard was tangled, matted, and greasy. Lice flecked the hair that hung long from the sides of his head, leaving the top of his head completely bald and rosy from the cold.

It was the man's eyes that held Longarm's gaze. They were almost yellow, like a wolf's, and every bit as wild.

Longarm held the man's head back against the door, and frowned. "Why?"

The man's eyes flashed, and he snarled, showing his chipped, yellow teeth. He tried to lift his large, scarred right hand, but he only got it up a few inches before it dropped back down to his thigh, and his jaw sagged, and the light flickered from his eyes. His bloody chest stopped rising and falling.

Longarm removed his rifle's butt from the man's head. His chin dropped to his chest.

A shadow slid across the killer's glistening bald pate.

Longarm heard a low, raspy breath beneath the wind's howl.

Oh, no, he thought.

There was the crunch of snow under a boot, and he whipped around to see a bulky figure filling the gray doorway, nearly totally blocking the light. The man wore a long, patched buffalo coat, the sour stench of which Longarm could smell from ten feet away, and a fox hat with loose earflaps. His long black hair blew around his bearded face in the wind as he pressed his cheek to the stock of the large-caliber, octagonal-barreled Sharps rifle in his hands. Squinting a coal-black eye to site down the barrel, planting a bead on Longarm's head, the man stretched his furred lips back from his teeth in a smile of raw, feral delight.

Ah, shit, Longarm thought, setting his jaws and awaiting the shot.

Something moved above and behind the man. The killer grunted and jerked forward. The big Sharps exploded, stabbing umber flames, and the large-caliber round screamed past Longarm's head to hammer the door flanking him.

Longarm's breath caught in his throat as he watched the man stumble toward him, as though exhausted after a long race. His knees gave, and he fell forward, dropping the rifle and hitting the floor on his face and chest, atop the rifle, only a foot or two in front of Longarm.

The lawman stared, his lower jaw hanging, at the shiny oak handle of the pickax jutting up from the killer's broad back. Blood welled up around the blade embedded deep in the man's coat.

Longarm lifted his gaze to see another figure filling the doorway. An inscrutable figure bundled against the weather, baggy denim trousers tucked into the tops of knee-high lace-up boots. A frost-rimed beard hung nearly to his belly.

The mute hermit, Herman Waverly, strode forward, stopped in front of Longarm. The lawman's heart skipped a beat, and his hand began sliding toward his pistol but froze when the newcomer reached down to wrap his fur-mittened hands around the pickax. Longarm saw the kind, intelligent eyes though the hermit's gaze did not meet his. Waverly merely planted one hobnailed boot against the dead man's back and pulled his pick from between the man's shoulder blades with a grunt and the ripping sound of torn flesh.

Hefting the weapon one-handed, the hermit turned and strode back out the door through which he'd entered. Beyond him, the big, bald gent, Scotty, was slogging through the snow, heading toward the depot building, a rifle in his arms. When Scotty saw the hermit angling off to his left, he stopped suddenly and leveled his rifle.

"Let him go!" Longarm shouted.

Striding heavily, feeling the fatigue in every bone and joint, he walked to the open door through which snow blew, swirling. He waved to the big man, who wore a heavy black stocking cap on his bald head, and who turned slowly to watch the hermit trudge off into the storm— heading for one of maybe several cabins he had around here.

Scotty turned toward Longarm as the lawman tramped toward him, his rifle on his shoulder. The bald gent scowled. "He ain't one of 'em?"

"He saved my damn bacon. Probably saved yours, too."

"That the last of 'em?"

Remembering Thunder Brodie and the events of the past thirty-six hours here in Sully Creek, Longarm chuckled darkly. "Let's sleep with one eye open till the storm passes."

He brushed past the still-scowling bald man, heading for the Trinity and a warm bed.

It wasn't long before he was nuzzling Janice Hathaway's large, warm breasts and jutting pink nipples near a popping, soothing fire . . .

And now he was toiling between her magnificent, spread legs, drowning the wind's maniacal howling with the Angel of the Rockies' impassioned sighs.

Watch for

LONGARM AND SHOTGUN SALLIE

the 378th novel in the exciting LONGARM
series from Jove

Coming in May!

GIANT-SIZED ADVENTURE FROM
AVENGING ANGEL LONGARM.

BY TABOR EVANS

2006 Giant Edition:

LONGARM AND THE
OUTLAW EMPRESS

2007 Giant Edition:

LONGARM AND THE
GOLDEN EAGLE SHOOT-OUT

2008 Giant Edition:

LONGARM AND THE
VALLEY OF SKULLS

2009 Giant Edition:

LONGARM AND THE
LONE STAR TRACKDOWN

penguin.com/actionwesterns

M456AS0409